I0712475

A Malitu Prequel Novella

Don't Bloody the Flag

JAMES LLOYD DULIN

G & D Publishing

First paperback edition January 2024

Cover Illustration by Martin Mottet
Typography by Michael Dulin
Map by Gustavo Schmitt
Copy Edit by Sarah Chorn

ISBN: 979-8-9871736-4-0 (paperback)
ISBN: 979-8-9871736-5-7 (hardcover)
ASIN: B0CQWWL5T3 (ebook)

www.jamesldulin.com

CONTENT AND TRIGGER WARNINGS
As a note of caution, this story contains depictions of graphic violence, war, death of loved ones, abusive parental figures, grief, trauma, and abandonment.

The world can be a distant place that separates us from each other.
I am fortunate and grateful to have my wife and partner, Aneicka, by my
side. My children, Sonny and Dominic, make this family complete.

Thank you.

ENNEA

TOLTÍAN
RENÉODA
NORTH ENOCH
ASTILE
PORT BILÁN
MYANACK
STRAITS OF TALMO
COLIAN
TOMAK
DASOON
NOMAR
TAL KINIC OCEAN
JAHIQUE
RONOPA
SONACOA
PROTISI
N

CHAPTER ONE

Isāla

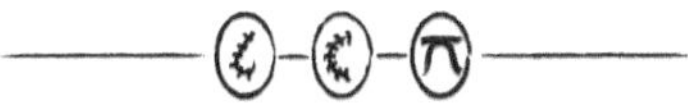

Peace isn't passive. How could it be? When violence cuts through the hearts of our people, how could peace have a chance waiting for them to come with bended knee and abandoned blade?

Wanti, founding member of the Clan

With a handful of unplanned words, Isāla had offered her blood. And why not? These never-ending wars had already claimed three generations of her kin.

If she didn't succeed now, the fighting would claim them all eventually.

As she sat on the swept dirt floor of her tent, she took stock of her supplies for a third time. Everything she needed and more lay out before her. It would all fit into a single travel sack—robes, saltmeat, waterskins, and a good flint rock. Nomadic life had taught her to pack well and travel light. Ennea, the land and The Mother, would provide the rest.

The leather canopy shook as her uncle, Mātan, threw the furs from the entrance and rushed in. Whatever violence he had known in his past settled in his furrowed brow, but his anger dissipated as he saw her travel supplies spread across the dirt.

"No," he said. It came out soft but definitive.

"I'm assuming you've already spoken to the elders." Because of course he had. Whatever ideals he might have carried, he had always made it clear she existed beyond them.

"Just because you convinced desperate people to let you get yourself killed," he said, gesturing emphatically with every word, "doesn't mean I'm going to shut my mouth and let it happen."

"I'm going, Uncle. I have to do this."

"Have to? Fiere died. Luc will be lucky if he only loses his arm."

As he spoke, the image of Luc stumbling back into the encampment, his robes stained red with his blood, flashed in front of her. They had grown up together, separated by only a handful of turns.

The elders should have sent her in the first place, but Mãtan had convinced them otherwise. Now, Fiere's body lay somewhere in the open expanse between the Sonacoan border and the northern coast of Tomak. Her jaw clenched at the needless violence of it.

"The wars are only getting worse, and you think now is the time for you to answer the Clan's ask?"

"The conclave is in less than two span," she said. "If the four nations aren't there, the first real peace talks in a century will end before beginning. How many nomads have gone to The Mist setting the groundwork for this one chance at peace? Their deaths have to mean something. Fiere's death has to mean something."

"That is not your responsibility!"

"That is all our responsibility!" Isãla yelled, her voice far louder than she had intended. "You taught me that."

Mãtan slumped to the ground and tore off his headwrap in the process, allowing his thick black curls to take up the space they were constantly denied. "I promised your mother I would keep you safe."

She winced, biting back her anger at the mention of her mother. "That was over twenty turns past. I'm not a little girl anymore."

His lips plumped into a mournful smile. "Promises don't have time limits. Not promises like that."

"I am not my mother or her choices."

"You don't know how much like your mother you are." Bitterness slipped into his tone.

There had been a time in her childhood when she yearned for such comparisons, but now the words took the shape of an insult. To be compared to a woman who had stayed behind to wage war—no one besides Mātan could have gotten away with it.

"Ever since you came of age, the elders have plotted to send the General back her daughter." He kept his face as neutral as possible, but his nostrils flared, betraying his anger. "'Who better to convince her of peace,' they said. Now, you go to them when I'm not around to say a word against it?"

"This is bigger than either of us. You know that."

"It was easier when you were younger." His shoulders slumped as he pinched the bridge of his nose. "You were just as stubborn, but at least I could pick you up."

"It's your fault. You taught me that being clan meant more than avoiding the violence."

A hollow chuckle fell from his lips like defeat. "I was foolish, and you were foolish for listening to me."

"If all four nations aren't represented at the conclave, the wars will continue. You know that. Which means I have seven days to make it to the shores of Renēqua." She closed the gap between them and placed a hand on his shoulder. "I don't want to live in world that known nothing but war."

"At least you'd be alive."

"Uncle, I need you to support me in this." And she did. There would always be a part of her seeking his approval—the young girl too scared to displease the only family she had left for fear of losing him too.

A silent moment stretched between them like clothes strung from a line, bowing until it could no longer take the weight.

"Where are your healing herbs?" Mátan asked, gesturing to her supplies.

"Thank you, Uncle."

"Thank me by coming home."

———

The River sang a storm on the horizon as Isála said her goodbyes. The spirit's call sounded of a promise—gentle tones reaching into The Song just enough to announce themselves before dissipating. Spirits had a way of foretelling danger with beauty.

Far too few amongst the Clan could hear and dance with The Song. The nations had higher priorities than to snuff out the nomadic bands of refugees and deserters, but dancers were different. Dancers were their weapons, and no nation at war could risk going into battle unarmed.

With the clarity of a new day and the weight of her task, The River seemed like such a small power compared to the war she was venturing into. What could water do against iron and steel?

"May The Great Spirits guide you," Elder Melin said as she pressed a leather pouch and a bundle of black fabric into Isála's hands.

"And may The Mother hold you well," Isála said in keeping with tradition.

"The flag will mark you as an envoy of peace and the missive is for your mother's eyes alone. If anyone else were to know the location of the conclave..." She shook her head. "The massacre that would follow if the wrong people got their hands on this information would promise another hundred turns of war."

"What if I can't trust the General with it?"

The older woman's lips tilted with sympathy that deepened the wrinkles in her ochre skin. "Young one, you are going to have to make that decision. And I, for one, trust you with it."

Isála wrapped her arms around Melin, who had always been

something of a grandparent where Isála'd had none.

As much as she had asked for the Clan to trust her, the moment felt too heavy for her to bear. The need to act pulled on her even as the fear ignited a fire within.

The simple length of black cloth and paper sealed within a leather pouch could change everything. Isála stowed them away before she lingered on the pressure of her mission too long.

Every farewell held too much finality. People she had known since her uncle brought her to the Clan twenty-three turns ago squeezed and fussed over her like this would be the last time they would meet this side of The Mist.

None of them voiced their concerns, but their doubts loomed over goodbyes and well wishes. She carried the weight of their futures.

If her spirit had to move on to The Mist to give peace a chance, so be it. At least that was what the stubborn voice at the back of her heart screamed despite her encroaching fear.

Ennea deserved better than the blood that soaked her soil, and her people deserved the opportunity to be more than warriors.

Mátan waited for the rest of the Clan to have their go before he came to her. "One last chance to abandon your principles and stick around here with me."

"Who else would they send? You're the only other person who can speak proper, and you move slower than your age."

A familiar false sternness transformed his features into a reprimanding mask. "Cha ain't speak proper since cha a baby girl."

"Don mean my tongue don rememer."

"Cha soun bout as silly as a fish tryin ta take ta sky from ta birds," Mátan said, then pulled her into a bone-crushing hug.

"You can list all the things that make you the right person to answer this ask, but they would never come close to the real reason," he said. "This isn't about your mother. You got a powerful spirit inside you, and I'm not talking about The River."

He bent down and pressed three fingers to the dirt before bringing them to his lips. "May The Mother be kind to whoever would dare try to stop you."

"Uncle, I..." Isāla started. "You have been my entire family all my life."

"You got your mother."

"No, I don't. I can't even remember what she looks like. I only ever had you," she said. "I love you."

Mātan reached around to the small of his back and pulled a long, curved knife from his belt, much bigger than anything meant to clean game or strip kindling. "I know you don't want to carry this, but I need you to."

"I know how to use my staff well enough."

"If someone means to kill you, you have to be ready to defend yourself," he said. "The ask is bigger than your scruples."

"You can't heal the bleeding with a blade."

"Stop." His voice dropped pitch. "Those sayings. Those teachings are the ground I have built my life upon, but sometimes life demands we sacrifice for something greater. You have seven days to get that letter to your mother. If you can't be ready to sacrifice everything to make that happen, you shouldn't go."

"Uncle..."

"Just say okay and take the knife."

Dark spots tarnished the metal along the blade, but it had been well cared for. The edge cut the morning light as it rested on Mātan's open palms.

"Okay," she said, and turned to let him tie the sheathed blade to her belt.

It rested on her thigh, a heavy betrayal of what she and the Clan stood for. Blood belonged to The Mother. It was not hers to take.

"Isāla," Teshun called from the other side of the encampment. "We need the light."

With a promise of peace stuffed in her travel sack and the threat of violence dangling from her hip, she took one last look at her uncle and the people who had raised her.

"Teshun and Rione are good people. They know the land. Listen to them, alright?"

Good people they might have been, but Isála didn't know them beyond niceties and a handful of stories—nomads amongst nomads, bouncing between one encampment to the next. They had a reputation for always answering when the Clan asked. They also had a reputation for returning bloody.

Why the Clan continued to rely on them despite their actions eluded Isála.

"May The Mother hold you," Isála said.

"I love you, kid. Now, get going before I think better of all this." Tears welled along Mátan's eyelids.

As she turned from her uncle, she knew nothing could take her from this path. Anything yet to come could only pale to the difficulty of the first footsteps she took away from him.

Clan had always meant several things depending on context. The interwoven networks of nomads and war refugees were clan. The twenty people Isála grew up with were clan. The people who bounced from encampment to encampment answering asks for the elders were clan.

Teshun and his sister, Rione, were the latter. Though, if not for their headwraps, Isála would have never known them for nomads. Their names always carried far too much blood for her taste.

On the few occasions the siblings had stayed in their encampment, Isála had kept her distance, never sharing more than basic pleasantries with them. If the stories were true, Teshun and Rione had far more in common with the armies of the four nations than they did with the Clan.

Of course, by some humor of the spirits, the siblings had been squatting on the edge of their encampment when Luc returned from his failed journey north. Now, Isāla would become part of their stories.

They trudged forward without a backward glance for her. Despite being shorter, Rione carried herself like the larger of the two. Her shoulders stretched her robes wider than the fabric's natural give. And the large onyx axes cradled on either hip didn't seem to slow her gait in the slightest. Unlike the knife bouncing against Isāla's thigh.

Rione's black axes were well known—stone met steel and refused to break. As if they were daemontales made real, Isāla stared at the killing stones. How many lives had they ended?

The heft of her stormwood walking staff helped calm her nerves. Even if her mettle threatened to bend under the weight of their journey and what it could mean, the stormwood would remain as strong as ever.

Rione and Teshun were more than capable of delivering a letter for the Clan. However, when borders erected around old ethnic lines, wars tended to imbue the enemy with specific features.

Their skin may have only been a few shades darker than Isāla's, but headwraps couldn't hide every strand of their characteristically Tomakan gray hair. Once they reached the shores of Renēqua, they would need someone who didn't look the part of an enemy.

So, for the first time in over twenty turns, Isāla would return to the island where she had been born.

"Do you think this will work?" Isāla asked, daring to breach the silence between them.

"You're going to have to be more specific," Rione said without breaking her stride. "Questions work best when they're specific. Try again."

"The conclave?" Isāla said with a bite to her words. "Do you think we can really do it?"

"We? My brother and I have been trekking our asses from coast to coast for the better part of two turns trying to make this work. I promise you; it wasn't for the scenery."

"What my kind-hearted sister means to say is yes, we believe in what we are doing. Treaties have failed before, but if we can bring all four nations together as one, peace has a chance. We believe that enough to have lost friends along the way and put ourselves in danger more times than I am comfortable counting."

Where Rione held herself apart, Teshun turned and smiled as he spoke. His smile not only carried through his words, but into his posture.

"Let's get this out of the way before anyone gets confused." Rione stopped and aimed her heavy attention at Isála, which made Isála wish Rione would go back to ignoring her. "We have given too much to fail now. The fact that your elders sent a couple of inexperienced kids north to deliver the missive to Renēqua in the first place pisses in the face of the dead and buried who got us this far. We are going to deliver you and that letter in your travel sack, and we'll see if the elders selected better this time around."

"We really should get going," Teshun said. "The scouting party from the west will only wait at the lodestone for so long before they have to move on."

"She's had her say. Now, it's my turn." Isála gripped her staff as hard as she could to keep her hand from shaking as she faced the nomad warrior. "I may not have seen what you've seen or lost what you've lost. But I've lost plenty. Ending the blood means as much to me as it does to you. Don't assume I am not here to fight."

One edge of Rione's mouth quirked into a sly smile. "We will see. Because mark my words, young one; before we are done, the spirits will weigh you. And so will I."

"I'm glad we could come to such a lovely understanding," Teshun said, returning to their path.

CHAPTER TWO

NOBEL

The King of Astile may or may not be a descendent of the first dancer as he claims. This does not make him The Shadow's chosen. This does not make him The Mother's chosen. Any claims that a single person should lead the entirety of Ennea, spit in the face of our history of collective efforts. Yes, we have known war, but we have also known great achievements when we have come together.

The Many Parts of Ennea, Baerro of Sonacoa

Nobel sat beside the fire with his two companions, each passing the time in the silence of their own company. He drew his blade down a leather strap, and the scraping gave rhythm to the waiting. The hours it took to care for his long knife allowed him time to think. With each stroke of the knife's edge, he sank deeper inward.

Clan from the furthest reaches of Ennea had seeded the battlefields for over two turns, and if all went well, their harvest would ripen in a matter of two span. A lowly bunch of refugees and deserters like himself bringing the nations to peace.

Yet, for all that effort, so much came down to the final days.

Missives were making their way to elders and leaders of every nation, informing them of the conclave's location. Even if they failed tonight, one of the elders from the west of Tomak had already agreed. As long as they could gather one representative from each nation, they had a chance. Though more would make the transition easier, especially given general Kaiut's bloody reputation.

It had to be done this way. Too many people with power would object. Some would arrive at the peace talks with blades.

Even as Nobel honed the edge of his knife, one that had spilled far too much Ennean blood, he yearned to put it down. But some people would never give up on old ideas.

Blood owed blood.

When people became too attached to their labels, they tended to forget their blood belonged to Ennea, The Mother. They forgot that there had been times when borders didn't exist.

Tomakan blood. Sonacoan blood. Astilean blood. Renêquan blood. All of it flooded back into The Mother's embrace, feeding her soil.

Since he abandoned his post in the Tomakan army a dozen turns past, Noble had answered asks for the Clan. If he hadn't made himself useful, he would have succumbed to his shame for the turns he spent following orders—killing strangers.

For the last two turns, he had come to visit Elder Sooni to convince her of a different path, one in which the four nations served Ennea rather than themselves.

"Two fingers to sunset," Murea said as she held her hand in front of her face, measuring the sun's fall. Her headwrap gathered the flickering firelight. "Elder should be here soon."

"Will you go home when the fighting's over?" Tralle asked from beside the fire.

"Home?" Nobel had been a different person when he absconded from Colian, Tomak's capital city, in the middle of the night after a particularly bloody engagement with Renêqua. Being this close to the city sent the cold crawling over his skin.

"I think the Clan will be home until The Mist welcomes me," he said.

"Me, I'm done with nomad life. Give me a bit of land and a few good seeds." Tralle grinned, and the turns faded from his face.

"You'd get bored after a season," Murea said. "There's too much to see to stick to one place for too long."

An inkling of jealousy crawled along Nobel's spine. Tralle had never served the Tomakan army like he and Murea had. His parents fled when he was still too young to serve.

The idea of finding a place to settle into life threatened Nobel's mind with nightmares. When he stayed in one place too long, his dead found him. The countless unnamed people he had cut down. Best to continue moving, even on tired legs.

But maybe Tralle had the right of it. If they could end the wars—truly end them—they would have to heal, not just the warriors, everyone. It would take time, but Enneans were capable of far more than they had become. Maybe they could make the ancestors smile on the other side of The Mist.

A pattern of three notes whistled into the forest, and Nobel tensed. The signal he had been waiting for, but the suddenness of it had him clutching his blade.

In many ways, the wars might never leave his bones, but he was willing to give time a chance to prove him wrong.

Nobel traded the hilt of his long knife for a hollowed-out length of wood and repeated the patterned notes he had heard.

Peace or not, all three nomads readied their weapons as the brush shifted.

The elder stepped to the edge of the firelight dressed in pale green robes, her gray braids bundled atop her head like a crown. Contrary to her title, Sooni wore her middle turns well. The last of Sokan's light set her red-brown skin aglow.

Colian sheltered far too many people to know them all, and Nobel had never encountered Sooni in his time there. But he would have liked to. Whatever reticence he had felt through their many clandestine meetings had always been tempered with a feeling of gravity towards the woman. Maybe that's why the people had lifted her to the elder's council.

Two guards flanked either side of the elder, swords in hand. The young man and woman barely had the turns to understand much beyond the orders they had been given. But at least they didn't have the weight of turns fighting a bloody war hovering over the proceedings.

"Elder Sooni, it's a pleasure to see you again," Nobel said, dropping his long knife to his side. He looked up to the sky and the pinks of sunset had given way to soft purples. "It's a beautiful night to speak of peace."

The Elder shook her head. "Why do you always say that? Thunder could be parting the sky, and you would still say the same thing."

"Thunder has more place on this land than war," he said. "And I think it's a more pleasant way to start a conversation than 'have you made up your mind yet?'"

She smiled before catching herself and forcing a more solemn expression to her face. "We have all lost too much to these wars, Nobel. If the other elders are willing to treat, I will listen to what they have to say." She spoke with the practice and weariness of her turns.

The next breath filled his chest with a warmth that ran contrary to the evening's chill. He had done it. The guilt that always weighed so heavily over his shoulders eased ever so slightly. "May The Great Spirits guide your heart."

When he reached for the leather-bound missive secured in his robes, he hesitated. The guard to Sooni's right gripped the hilt of his sword in a way that set his arm trembling. The warrior may have been young, but everyone's weapons had been lowered. They had met before. Something had set his spirit on edge.

"And may The Mother hold you well," Elder Sooni said in return.

"I hope you appreciate our precautions," Nobel said, removing a folded piece of paper from his satchel, hoping the others had picked up on his coded warning. "Secrecy is of the utmost importance."

As soon as Sooni clutched the piece of paper, she retreated from the light. Something resembling regret pulled at her brow. A tight whistle cut through the air from behind the nomads followed by an arrow. It barely missed Murea before sinking into a tree.

The forest cloaked their enemy's numbers, but Nobel still had both of Sooni's young guards in sight.

So much for healing old wounds, Nobel thought as he flung his secondary belt knife at the guard with the trembling hand. The blade pierced the man's thick thigh as he bellowed into the night.

Murea swept her feet into a wide stance as her hands curved and curled over one another. The night stilled before a torrent of wind careened through the outcropping, throwing Sooni and her guards to the ground.

"Retreat!" Murea called, but her tongue failed to find the final consonant as she fell face-first into the firepit with an arrow protruding from her neck.

"No!" Nobel screamed, as stared at his lifeless friend.

For all his rhetoric of forgiveness and healing, the bloodlust of his youth claimed him as he rushed towards the downed guards, brandishing his long knife.

Murea had been the person who found him after he escaped the army. She had helped him find his path through his anger and resentment. If anyone deserved to see the other side of peace, she did.

Before he could reach the guards, the air in front of him glimmered with a familiar sheen.

A fire dancer. The thought formed in his mind as the odd pocket of air filled with heat then burst in a flash of flames.

Heat crawled over his exposed flesh, spots of light dotted his visions, and the forest floor tumbled over the night sky. When his body came to a rest, he lay on his back next to his dead friend, the fire crawling across her body.

She deserved better. Murea had only ever tried to put this world back together, but the fuckers were determined to shatter whatever peace they could find.

More arrows cut through the night, but everything had gone silent. Somewhere in the shadows of the forest, the cowardly fire dancer waited to finish them.

"Run, Tralle," he tried to say, but the words failed to fight through the back of his throat.

"You said you wouldn't hurt them. They are only trying to end the bloodshed." Elder Sooni's voice sounded distant and small.

"Traitors get no quarter, Elder. You would do well to remember that," a nameless voice said. "Do you have the location?"

Paper ruffled, and Nobel smiled. The movement probably should have hurt. He felt his skin resist and crack with the pull of his cheeks, but the pain only came through as an ever-present sting throughout his body—hollow and empty in the way it consumed the whole of him.

"What the fuck is this!" the voice bellowed.

With the last of his strength, Nobel ripped the missive from its leather pouch concealed within his robes.

Feet scuffled over the dirt. "No," the disembodied voice called out.

A hand clutched his wrist, but it was too late. Nobel had already removed the letter and fed the paper to the firepit beside him.

"You're going to regret that." The owner of the voice loomed over Nobel, a twenty-something Tomakan man with gray braids patterned along his scalp. Far too pretty a face to have seen much of the wars.

Peace may not have come tonight, but it hadn't died either. Murea's spirit could rest easier knowing that.

"Tantin, take two warriors with you and track down the deserter," the young warrior ordered.

If Nobel found The Mist tonight, he could do so with a smile, knowing there was still a chance for Tralle and the conclave.

CHAPTER THREE
NOBEL

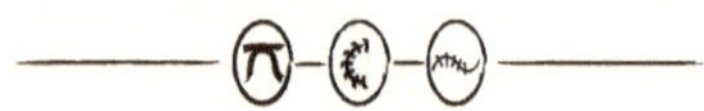

Few things separate into clear boundaries. The Mother is the giver of life. She is the land. She is matriarch to the sun and moons, the spirits great and small. The inherent ambiguity in her defines people as well. We are violent, craven animals who love deeply and want to outshine the flaws we carried yesterday. If we fail because we choose to see the potential in imperfect people, we have succeeded in taking a step closer to who The Mother made us to be.

In Our Nature, Tamlis of the Clan

All day, The Song had carried a storm in its voice. It grew with the hours until The River only knew the impending fall. Then The Song sang of relief, subtle sweet melodies of water returning to the earth.

Isála loved rainstorms.

The water allowed her to see the world beyond what her eyes could glean as it dripped and settled around her. It fed the soil, and the forest swelled with its gift.

Of course, her companions preferred to take shelter beneath a leather canopy for the night.

If she wanted to, she could stop the rain with a simple dance—contort The River and ask the clouds to hold their form above. But

The Waking moved in harmony with the spirits, and calling them to manipulate the world for shallow comforts went against everything the Clan had taught her.

So she rested against a tree in the relative dryness they had crafted for themselves beneath the stitched-leather shelter.

Rione had fallen asleep immediately after their meager meal of apples and saltmeat. As the firelight flickered over her, all the bravado and weight of her presence diminished.

"She isn't so scary when she's sleeping, is she?" Teshun asked with his back pressed against a tree on the other side of the fire.

"The two of you don't seem like siblings at all."

"We get that a lot." His hands drifted over his lap, carrying an odd rhythm to their movement. "People and their expectations get in the way of them being able to see the ways in which we are alike."

"Which are?"

"Beyond our obvious charm and good looks?"

The night may have obscured her rolling eyes, but she couldn't help herself. "Of course, beyond the obvious," she said as dryly as she could.

Teshun smiled. "Story as old as the wars, I'm sure. Our father is a Tomakan warrior, at least he was the last time we saw him. By rights and time alone, he should have found a bit of command. He's not a bad fighter, has a decent head on his shoulders, but his mouth is too quick for his better judgement. We both got that from him.

"But the more responsibilities and opportunities passed him by in favor of younger, less-capable warriors, the more bitter he became. Rione got tough. I got good at talking my way out of a spot. It all comes from the same place. I guess you could say we got that from him too."

"You don't hold anything back, do you?"

"If you want to talk about the rain or how much you enjoy the spring, I'm happy to. But the way I see it, we are either going to die together or achieve something more important than any of us will ever fully understand. So why be coy? We all have our damages."

"Your damages are much more pleasant than your sister's."

Teshun's hands froze in the middle of their dance, and he turned his focus to Isála. "Don't. Don't test my good nature. My sister is off-limits. Understood?"

"All I said was…"

"I heard what you said, and I said what I said. Just don't." His attention and hands went back to their work, but the looseness in his shoulders didn't return as easily.

"My mother was a warrior the last time I saw her too," she said, like an offering.

He stopped moving his hands and met her eyes again. "The General. The elders told us all about it. Only reason Rione didn't complain louder about bringing you."

"I'm more than her daughter," Isála said. "Barely remember the woman. She left me with my uncle when I was four. My brother and father had just died in a raid, and she left me to go back to war."

"Why are you telling me this?"

"Like you said, we're in this shit together. Might as well be honest."

He chuckled despite the still-present tension in his shoulders. "I think I lent my words a bit more eloquence than that."

"What are you doing over there?" She mimicked his dancing hands.

The silence between them persisted long enough to twist her gut. Maybe she had said something wrong again. Then he waved her over.

The soft streams of light that cut through the storm and forest shuttered on the reflective surface of a small black stone in his lap. As he moved his hands to the part of The Song that belonged to The Mountain, the edges of the stone eroded and weathered away.

Earth dancers were capable of far larger feats, shifting rock and stone beneath the soil, crumbling buildings in a matter of moments. Whatever time, force, and pressure could make of stone and earth, they could make happen almost instantaneously.

But this simple, subtle grinding down of stone seemed beneath his capabilities.

"Couldn't you just grind down the stone's edge with a couple of tools?"

"It's onyx, and I thought you were a dancer," he said. "Try looking a bit closer."

Bits of eroded onyx fell from the stone to a pile below as one side of the stone slimmed to an edge. The shape of the stone shifted ever so slightly. What was she missing?

"Where's the rest of the stone?" The falling debris couldn't account for the changing shape. Not all of it.

"There you go."

The firelight reflecting off the stone bent as one side of the onyx shifted.

"You're compressing the stone? You can do that?"

"Come on. You've heard the stories. I've seen you looking at my sister's axes. There's a reason they stand up to iron and steel," he said with a self-assured smile. "Beneath the surface of the earth, pressure naturally compresses stone. The toughest gemstones are made of the same things as everything else, with a bit more time and pressure."

The edge grew thinner and sharper as his hand danced over the stone.

In theory, she could do something similar with ice, but never to the same extent. Mátan had tried to teach her, but the idea of making blades always crept too close to deadly violence for her.

"Why not use iron and steel instead?"

"First off, neither of us is a blacksmith. Second, the blades I make will outlive whatever metal you throw at them. Last, and most important, have you seen those axes? As beautiful as they are deadly, if I say so myself."

Minutes stretched as Isála watched the stone compress and erode. The edges gleamed in what little light they shared, forming a small knife with an even smaller hilt.

"What good is something like that?"

He cradled the half-finished knife in his hand, then flicked his wrist, and a subtle thunk cut through the storm. "I've never been any good at what you'd call close combat." Teshun opened a leather pouch at his hip, revealing a dozen more knives. "Want to try?"

"No, thanks. I have my staff."

"See, that's why we don't like to travel with clan brats. No offense, but you don't know anything outside the safety of your clan. Aversion to violence doesn't work out here. What happens when it's between your life and someone else's? You know what delivering that letter could mean. Are you going to let your purity stop you from ending this fighting?"

Isála sat back at the comment with a soft anger kindling in her gut. "No offense?"

"Yeah, it's just the truth."

"The truth is you can't create peace by killing people."

"Who says?" Teshun plucked another onyx stone from the pile beside him. "It's a pretty turn of phrase and all that, but sometimes people are barriers to peace."

"Then you go around them," she said, her voice cutting sharper than she intended.

He chuckled. "I like you, Isa. You got a quick tongue, but inaction can kill as easily as a blade. The elders might not like to admit it, but they rely on people like my sister so they can keep their values nice and shiny."

As his hands went back to work, Teshun leaned back against a tree. His chani cloth headwrap covered his hair like any other nomad's. He had been taking on asks for the Clan for turns. But he was just as much a part of the wars as Isála's mother, taking blood for whatever cause they deemed worthy.

Why could none of them see how their pain only traveled downhill when they killed? How many of them picked up a sword because of the violence some unnamed warrior had done to their family? Not Isála. She wouldn't be responsible for spilling more blood. It already saturated the soil.

Chapter Four

Isála

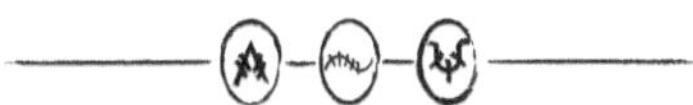

The leaders of each nation may be pursuing war in an effort to gather power and resources, but the warriors on the frontlines do not care. They do not fight for the metal in the mountains, the rich soil in the flatlands, or the bountiful timber of the forests. They fight because those that came before them gave their blood so the next generation could thrive. Right or wrong, those warriors believe in the debt they owe the dead. Blood owes blood.

Mindsets of a Warrior, Hánim of Renéqua

The Clan raised a series of lodestones across Ennea where they held the first peace talks with representatives from each nation. Warriors would give their blades to the naturally magnetic stones in a symbolic commitment not to spill blood.

To most people, the lodestones represented shelter from the violence plaquing Ennea.

The cylindrical column looked exactly as Isála had remembered it, black as the night sky, jutting out from the soil in the middle of a forest clearing. A downed ironoak rested where she had sat waiting with her mother so many turns ago.

The memory went blurry at the edges. Isála had been so full of questions that day.

As she, Teshun, and Rione approached, she removed her uncle's knife from its sheath and allowed the stone's pull to take the blade in accordance with tradition. For all she knew, it was the same knife her uncle gave to the stone the day he came to collect her.

"The best thing about carrying stone weapons is not having to give them up for silly traditions," Rione said, clinking an axe against the lodestone to no effect.

"Why do you insist on mocking everything the Clan stands for like you aren't clan yourself?" Isála tossed her travel sack to the ground, turning on the warrior nomad.

"What my sister meant to say…"

"Shut it, Tesh. I don't need you speaking for me." Rione squared her shoulders towards Isála. "I'll give you the benefit of the doubt because you have lived your entire life sheltered from the wars, but you'll need to learn quick that the world speaks in violence more often than not. I'm not putting aside my blades because of some tradition. Not when it might mean the difference between survival and a quick trek to The Mist."

Whatever stories Teshun had spun about his not-so-little sister the night before meant nothing in this moment.

"Why are you here if you care so little for clan ways? There's no peace in blood."

"That's where you're wrong. You can regurgitate all the clan doctrine you've swallowed over your short turns, but it won't make it true. All the elders do is talk about peace. Do you see them here?" Rione gestured around her with wide arms. "No, they send people who know bloodshed to deliver their missives because they understand what is required, even if they don't want to admit it."

"That's why you volunteered, huh? You came out here looking for blood?" Isála gripped her staff tighter as her heart thumped in her ears alongside The River. "You're no better than all those bastards fighting to balance their debts."

"That's the dirty little secret, isn't it? I'm not. And neither are you, you little shit. The Clan's ever-present superiority doesn't make them better than the people fighting for their lives on the frontlines. Blood and violence aren't some fucking abstractions to muse about from the safety of the Clan."

Teshun took a step forward. "Shouldn't we all take a moment to..."

"Shut it, stone carver," Isāla said. The River sang a hurricane and begged her to dance with it. Every droplet of water from the soil to the vapor in the air called to her. "It's easy to go through life without principles and rail against those who believe in something."

"Believe in something? You don't know enough about the world to believe in anything. You're just spouting the piss and shit they fed you."

"You don't belong on these sacred grounds?" The Song reflected her rage and in turn, fed it. She grasped her staff between both hands, channeling her anger into the sturdy wood.

"There we go. Let it out. I've always wanted to see how stormwood holds up to onyx." Rione swung one of her axes free from its cradle on her hip.

Teshun rushed towards his sister, but she sent him stumbling back with a simple push.

"Don't worry, I won't hurt her much. But she has a lesson or two to learn in violence."

The clouds above gathered their moisture as Isāla moved her staff with The Song's pull.

"Help!" A Tomakan man wearing bloody robes and a disheveled headwrap burst through the brush into the clearing.

The rhythm of The Song lost its beat and stumbled as the man collapsed to his knees with an arrow protruding from his shoulder.

Teshun bent low to the earth and closed his eyes as if straining to hear something in The Song. "More coming."

"Get him to safety," Rione hissed at her brother as she pulled her second axe from its cradle. "Time to see how far your principles take you, little nomad."

"Is now really the time?" Teshun said, dragging the now collapsed man to the far edge of the clearing.

An odd flickering filled the gaps between the ironoaks where Isála had expected pursuers. Then, as if they rose from the soil, flames surged through the clearing followed by a barrage of arrows.

Before her feet could move, Rione grabbed her by the arm and forced her from the fire's path.

A slate of imperfect stone erupted from the earth, shielding them from flames and arrows, as Teshun beat his fists against the dirt.

Everything happened in an instant, and none of Isála's training could make sense of the scene. Her arms felt weightless as if she had just woken from a hard sleep.

Waves of heat washed over her as the flames swept through the clearing. The poetry of dying in the same spot where her mother had abandoned her added a bitterness to her fear.

Rione screamed beside her, but the sound lacked focus. It blended into the raging fires.

Isála would fail. And peace would fail with her.

The older nomad grabbed her by the shoulders and shook her. "Call The River!"

Words formed with Rione's moving lips, but they lacked meaning.

Flames engulfed the ringed clearing, growing closer and hotter. Then the world froze as Isála found the lodestone standing amongst the inferno like a solitary mourner for the safe haven it had once represented.

This place signified a small promise of peace amid far too much violence and chaos. And their attackers couldn't even respect that.

Rage flared in Isála's chest hotter than any flame, and The River sang a war song. She swept the earth with one foot as the other held her steady. With a single hand, she clutched all the waiting water in the sky and tore it from its resting place.

The midday vanished behind a torrent of rain, and the flames smoldered to suggestions of smoke.

Rione rushed past Isāla before her consciousness pulled itself separate from the clouds above. The waterlogged nomad brandished her axes and crashed into two would-be assassins dressed in the red robes of the Tomakan army. As she drew back her onyx axe, water sputtered off the weapon. Then stone clattered against metal.

A third Tomakan warrior rushed in to flank Rione, but Isāla's rage had not run its course. The Song filling her with purpose; she met the spear brandishing warrior before he had a chance to interrupt Rione's battle.

Water weighed down her robes, but it would not disrupt her course. In a movement as fluid as The River themselves, she pinned the blade of his spear to the ground with one end of her staff, slamming the other end into the side of his head.

The contact felt satisfying, as if it were the only way to quench a deep thirst within.

When the warrior found steady feet, he used the spearpoint to keep distance between the two of them. It was a sound strategy as he recovered from her first attack, but she had trained all her life under her uncle.

Mātan may have abandoned the war, but the war never left his bones.

When they spoke of violence, he pushed her understanding of what could be achieved outside of blood. Then he trained her to defend herself from physical violence as fervently as he taught her to resist its pull.

In these small moments, as the warrior collected his wits, Isāla reached for the better part of her spirit. Her rage could win this battle one way, but she refused to be subject to anger.

Rainwater dripping down her face, she mirrored her attacker's footwork and waited for a moment to break his guard.

He lunged forward, jabbing his spear over her shoulder. An opening. She carried the spearpoint higher with a twist of her staff, closed the distance, and slammed the other end of the stormwood into his gut.

Shouts and yelps broke out behind her, but she had to trust Rione would handle her fight. If she didn't, Isála would be a spirit ready for The Mist either way.

As her opponent buckled, he dropped his spear and lashed out with a long knife like the one her uncle had given her. It brushed over her arm in a blaze of heat, but it would not deter her. She swept her staff through his forward foot, setting him stumbling for balance, then brought the full weight of her stormwood across his face.

The light flitted in and out of his eyes before he fell slack against the earth.

She stared down at him, and a chill coursed through her that had nothing to do with the rain saturating her clothing.

"Well done," Rione said from over Isála's shoulder.

"Blessed fucking Mother!" Isála nearly jumped out of The Waking when she saw Rione. "What are you doing?"

"I finished with mine." Rione pointed to the bloody bodies behind her.

"You spilled blood beside the lodestone?!"

The rain dissipated as Rione stood there without shame.

"Get away from this man!" Isála grabbed him by the collar of his robes and dragged him to a nearby tree.

The bastard was no older than her—his skin taut with youth. Had she stayed in Renéqua, this was who she would have become: another warrior following orders. Maybe she would have lived long enough to give them.

After stripping him of one last knife, she bound him to an ironoak with his own belt.

Trees around the clearing wore soot and ash crawling up their trunks. The lodestone grounds were drinking the blood of the slain warriors.

Here I had assumed I had already experienced my bleakest moments beside this lodestone, she thought. I need to get far away from this place.

"I could use some help over here," Teshun called out.

Isála had forgotten about the injured nomad in the rush of the battle. She sprinted across the sodden dirt to help Teshun.

Resting against the stone barrier Teshun had pulled from the earth, the nomad shuttered with each breath. His eyes moved unnaturally slow before finding her.

"I don't think he's going to make it," Teshun said.

"General Kaiut," he coughed. "Nobel burned the letter, but he was still alive when I escaped."

"It's over," Teshun said.

"What are you talking about?" Isála asked. "There are elders in the west. Tomak will be at the talks. The mission to Colian was about bringing more voices to the table."

"If Kaiut finds out where the conclave is, no one will be safe," Teshun said.

"Nobel...won't give...in." The rasp in the man's voice overtook his words.

"Ennea, Blessed Mother, guide this spirit to you," Isála said.

"Tralle...my name is..." He shuttered with one final breath before his head slumped against the stone barrier.

Teshun sat back and looked to the sky. "We need to warn the others before it's too late. If Kaiut kills the delegations coming to the conclave, these wars will never end."

"Great Spirits, please be the peace Tralle didn't find this side of The Mist." She closed his eyelids, brought three fingers to her lips, then touched them to the wet soil.

"You're not listening to me. There is no more conclave. The mission has changed now."

"Let's see if Kaiut knows anything before we break turns of planning on a hunch." Isála pushed herself up from where she sat.

Across the clearing, the tied-up warrior hung limp against his bindings, blood running down his chest.

"What did you do?" The air fell out of Isála's lungs as she spoke.

"What you wouldn't," Rione said, wiping the blood from her axes. "If you let him go, he would have spilled more blood, caused more damage."

"That's not yours to decide. We aren't trying to save innocent bystanders. We are trying to save everyone, including the guilty ones."

"If we are going to sit down and talk about how everything should work, then I whole-heartedly agree with you," Rione said, sliding the handles of her axes back in their cradles. "But sometimes we have to make difficult calls. Sometimes we have to decide who dies before we give that power to the wrong person. Because until the conclave brings the nations to some agreement, peace is nothing more than a pretty idea."

"Did you even find out what he knew? Did you ask a single question before you slit his throat?"

"We have our friend over there to fill us in."

"No," Isála said. "We don't."

The words stopped meaning anything at some point. People who convinced themselves they understood how the world worked didn't hear anything that ran contrary. So Isála walked over to the lodestone and prayed for the spirits to show her a path forward.

———

Isála held her tongue as Teshun called on The Mountain. They carried the bodies from the clearing and gave them to The Mother before Teshun shifted the earth once again, covering the graves.

The rain had washed away most of the gore from Isála's hands, but it hadn't cleaned the bloody soil from her fingernails.

She prayed as the siblings conspired.

Maybe she had been too naïve, believing she could help peace. The first time she left her uncle's protection, she had desecrated a promised safe haven.

It had to mean something. She couldn't let the conclave die here.

Isála brought three fingers to her lips, then placed them on the dirt.

"Great Spirits, be my guide."

Wearing wet and bloody robes, she pushed herself from the ground and strode past the bickering pair of nomads. She still had six days to deliver the Clan's message to the Renéquans, and that was what she meant to do.

When she pulled her uncle's knife from the lodestone, the incessant chatter stopped. "What are you doing?" Teshun asked.

"I have a message to deliver."

"I can't decide how I feel about you," Rione said. "One minute you're bitching about principles, and the next you're making far more sense than this coward."

"Making the most logical decision based on what we know isn't being a coward!"

"Nobel doesn't even know what's in the missive."

"How can you be sure?"

"It doesn't matter. I told you. I know him. He's not going to talk. Nothing's changed." Rione picked up her travel sack. "Are you ready?"

"This is ridiculous…"

"Teshun, I understand you know how to talk your way in and out of situations, but this isn't one of those times," Isála said. "We answered the Clan, and I intend to follow through. You can stay behind, or you can stop talking and move."

"It's weird because you're being disrespectful to my brother right now, yet I'm starting to like you even more. I'm very conflicted."

With the weight of her uncle's knife safely back on her hip, Isála turned north. They may have had six days, but if they pushed themselves, they could cross the Strait of Talmo in five.

CHAPTER FIVE

LAIKEN

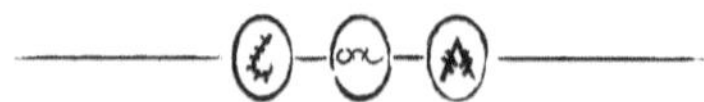

The Waking and The Mist are not as separate as one may think. Dancers are but the fortunate individuals who can hear one half of the whole calling the other. A wise person might realize then that our spirits are all a part of this call and response, that our spirits, though residing in different bodies, are not as separate as one may think.

Letter to the King of Astile, Astilean Elder Osin

Blood smeared the stone floors of the prison cell as Laiken laid the nomad against the far wall. His headwrap had fallen to the wayside during their travel, revealing gray braids neatly lining his scalp. The burn he had left across the man's face had begun to crack, creating layers of texture and color. The nomad could have been a good warrior.

What a waste of good Tomakan stock, Laiken thought.

Of course, the man would die in these walls, but Laiken felt a begrudging respect for him. Even as he straddled the edge of The Mist, he had managed to burn the letter Laiken had come to collect. That level of commitment to a cause was worthy of honor, even if the cause was not.

"Bring this man water and a blanket," Laiken said to the guard, who was barely old enough to carry a blade. He nodded before rushing from the room. "Don't worry, my friend. You will find The Mist soon. But first, my father will have questions for you."

Laiken situated himself next to the nomad, resting his back against the same wall. "If you look at it in a certain light, your clan is just another army working towards another cause. We are brothers on opposing sides of a line."

The Flame whistled in the distance like a lone candle in a great hall. It flickered and wavered as it consumed the wax around it, longing to be more. The same longing settled in Laiken's gut.

"I hold no ill will for you, brother. You did as commanded and made your people proud, I'm sure. But when my father arrives, for your sake, answer his questions. You need not suffer before joining the spirits."

The door pushed open as General Kaiut walked in, broad and imposing as ever.

"Father." Laiken clambered to his feet and adjusted his robes. "The prisoner has yet to speak."

"I'll take it from here." If anyone else were to hear Kaiut's words, they wouldn't glean the underlying meaning of his flattened tone. But Laiken was all too familiar with the slight alterations in his father's voice and stepped from the cell without another word.

His father grabbed a chair from the other side of the bars and sat it beside the prisoner.

"I'm sorry for my son's overzealousness," he said, and the tone of the apology touched on a truth. "You do not deserve the pain you are in."

The nomad remained still, save the rise and fall of his chest. Then his eyes shifted to meet Kaiut's.

"We are not enemies, you and I. My enemies have armies and weapons. You know this. You may have joined the nomads, but the spirits still mark you as Tomakan as any of us."

The door swung open as the young guard returned with a bucket and a blanket.

"Yes, thank you. If we need anything else, my son will call for you."

The guard stood at full height, back as straight as the iron bars of the cell, and nodded to the General before leaving once again.

Laiken watched in silence as his father collected the bucket and blanket. The General, who had held the Strait of Talmo for twenty turns, unfolded the meager blanket and draped it over his captive gingerly.

"Burns steal the heat from a body. You deserve as much comfort as we can give you." He dipped a cloth in the bucket and dabbed it gently over the man's burns. The man closed his eyes as Kaiut wiped the blood that clung to his skin.

"Would you give me your name? I gain nothing in your name but the honor of knowing it."

The nomad opened his mouth to cough, and Kaiut allowed him the time to find his voice.

"Nobel," he said in a voice without breath.

"Nobel. It's a good name. I, as you may have guessed, am General Kaiut, and that is my son, Laiken."

As his father spoke his name, Laiken winced. The General had placed his faith in Laiken's hands, and he had returned with a broken nomad instead of his intended prize.

"I have no wish to cause you pain. You have taken nothing from me or my people. In fact, I still consider you my people," Kaiut said. "But there are certain things I have to know. The Clan would rather a superficial peace to the honesty of war.

"I have too many families who have lost kin and land. Tomak stands alone at the center of these wars, and these trespasses cannot go unanswered. Surely, you understand. Something drove you to the Clan. Some loss."

The General picked up a second cloth, dipped it in water, and brought the cloth to Nobel's lips. A stream of water fell to the nomad's cracked lips. "Slowly," Kaiut cautioned.

As Nobel swallowed, his eyes closed and the tension in his jaw shook with the fight to bury the sounds of his pain.

"Blood owes blood, Nobel. A truer thing has never been spoken this side of The Mist." Despite Kaiut's smile, his anger seeped into his words. "As general, that debt settles in my spirit. My people—our people—look to me to answer for blood owed.

"Tell me where the Clan is hosting their peace talks. I need you to help me make sure our people have a chance to respond for the lives taken from them."

Nobel's eyes shifted from Kaiut to Laiken and back. "No."

With no further preamble, Kaiut ripped the knife from his belt and drove it through Nobel's foot with enough force to break the tip of the blade on the stone beneath.

Pain sent Nobel spasming in a noiseless scream as he reached for the wound, to no avail.

Kaiut pushed Nobel's back against the wall with the flat of his palm as he retrieved his knife. "I have no desire to hurt you further. I respect that you've made pledges to the Clan or whatever they asked of you, but I need what I need."

Finding his full voice for the first time, Nobel turned to the general. "I'm not telling you a fucking thing." The words rasped from the back of his throat as clear as possible.

"Know that you chose this path, deserter." Kaiut grabbed the nomad's hand and sliced into the skin between his thumb and pointer finger with the broken blade, eliciting a scream that filled the cell. "A Tomakan lowering himself to this false peace! Do you think the Astileans will keep to their borders? We have taken too many of their people and they too many of ours. Talk will not end this. I will."

Laiken clenched his fists as he watched his father torture the man he had taken prisoner. If he looked away, even for a moment, his father would punish him for the weakness. The scar across his palm burned with the memory of the last time he had lost his steel.

With each cut, Nobel's cries of pain grew weaker, and he slumped deeper. He ceased moving until the next cut jarred him from his slow fading. Kaiut knew how and where to cut to stretch the time before Nobel crossed over.

After his father finished cutting the webbing between Nobel's fingers, he began carving small pieces of flesh from his arms, pausing before each cut to ask the same question. "Where are the peace talks?"

Laiken had made excuses to other warriors, saying that his father hadn't been this way before his wife and eldest son died in a skirmish with Astile. And it held truth to it. The losses had carried General Kaiut's abusive tendences further towards the surface. But they had always been there behind enough barley wine.

Kaiut slapped his hand against the wall over Nobel's head, and the sound echoed through the chamber. "Renéqua sits across that strip of water, waiting for the opportunity to take what is ours! Our blood! Our land! I have lost too many warriors! Too many kin! You really think the other nations are considering putting down their weapons? How many treaties have they broken before? No. That is not the way those bastards work. They won't stop until there is no more blood to take."

He leaned to his prisoner's unblemished ears. "I will do what I have to do to protect mine, deserter."

Nobel met Kaiut's glare, his chest heaving arrhythmically.

"Did you notice anything about this building when my son brought you to the outpost? Anything that set it apart from the others?" Kaiut asked.

Sitting in a puddle of his own blood, Nobel looked up and found Laiken's eyes. His gaze was soft, almost pleading. Laiken had known what his father would do, and in that way, each scream wrenched from Nobel belonged to him as well.

"This is the only entirely stone building on the grounds." Kaiut's voice lowered to a whisper. "I'm not going to make you guess why. It's so the flames don't spread when we burn the bodies."

The dying man snapped to attention, and the plea in his eyes became a begging, but Laiken remained silent.

"If you want us to give your body to The Mother—bury you properly—you're going to tell me what I want to know."

Laiken returned Nobel's gaze with a plea of his own. He had no desire to desecrate the nomad's body and keep his spirit from finding safe passage to The Mist. But if ordered, he would. He had before.

"Laiken, get ready to call The Flame," Kauit said, still staring at Nobel. "We may need to cleanse this cell."

"I never read the letter." Blood dripped from Nobel's lips as he spoke. "The elders didn't want any of us to know what it said if someone caught us."

General Kaiut gave a small chuckle. "Smart. No, that's really smart. Nobel, I tell you, you would have made an excellent warrior. I don't begrudge your commitment for a moment, though it is to the wrong cause. If you want to find The Mist. I'm going to need you to give me something."

"Blessed Mother, forgive me." The nomad cradled his mangled hands and closed his eyes. "There are envoys traveling to Renéqua as we speak. We were set to meet them at the lodestone to the southwest this morning."

Beneath the blood and burns, the look of defeat on Nobel's face settled in Laiken's memory. It would be there until the day he died.

"Good. Good." Kaiut patted the nomad's head and brushed back his braids. "You did the right thing."

Kaiut held the nape of Nobel's neck and plunged the broken-edged dagger into his heart, watching as the last remnants of tension in Nobel's body eased.

Laiken's father stayed there beside the dead man for a moment, looking down at the lifeless body. Whatever Nobel had done at cross-causes with their own, he hadn't deserved this.

General Kaiut rose, wiping his hands with the blood-red rag, and moved to meet his son on the other side of the bars.

"I gave you a simple task and more than enough warriors to do it." He stepped uncomfortably close. "You could have avoided all this mess. Now, we have more work to do."

Pain crashed across Laiken's jaw as his father smacked him with his meaty palm.

"I don't have to tell you how important it is that we intercept those envoys, do I?"

"No, General."

Kaiut gave a slight smile and a nod. "Good. Now, clean up this mess. Then, get your ass out there and clean up your other mess. The Mother save me, I will balance our blood. Those nomadic bastards won't steal that from us."

The echoing footsteps of General Kaiut's boots against the stone floors filled the room before the door closed behind him, leaving Laiken in silence.

Pieces of Nobel lay in the pool of blood surrounding his body. Laiken stared off into an odd corner of the cell, steeling himself for the task at hand. For all of his father's words of care and respect at the end, he left his knife buried to the hilt in Nobel's chest.

The first step Laiken took towards the gruesome scene made him buckle at the waist and dry heave. Shit, blood, and burned flesh mingled in the air.

When he collected himself, he took another step towards the body, and another. He had to give Nobel back to The Mother. He owed the nomad that much. Not for his father's orders, but because some things were simply owed between brothers of war.

Chapter Six

Isála

*The nations were born out of a need to protect families. Where one family could
be taken advantage of, two families could resist. Bonds grew. Promises forged
forever larger families until borders were drawn, and people separated themselves.
The one people The Mother meant us to be became corrupted just like the once
worthy goal of protecting each other.*

*There is but one Waking and one Mist. Ennea has never and will never be four
separate pieces on a map, no matter how stubborn we are.*

A Treatise for Peace, Clan Elder Innra

Five Tomakan warriors clad in leather bracers and red robes swept through
the valley below, following the trail of the First Daughter's dying light. Isála
should have been afraid, but they were too much of a curiosity.

The pack of them moved over the land like scouts, but carried far too
much iron and steel. The third hunting party in two days. At least that's
what Rione had called them.

Isála breathed with The River as the spirit filled The Song with a
heaviness. Water moved with ease, but nothing could displace the

immensity of the ocean—ever-shifting in its permanence. This truth filled The Song.

With all likelihood, these warriors had lost people to the fighting. There were those who would mourn them should they not return.

It didn't make sense.

If the wars ended, they could return home and put down their blades. They could share a life with their remaining loved ones. Even so, they stalked over the countryside, trying to kill a chance for peace.

Somehow, the strange lines the nations had drawn through the land made these people, Isála's people, Enneans, forget the bonds they shared.

One of the warriors wore her gray hair shorter than the others. Her curls puffed up in a crown around her head, accenting her sharp cheekbones. If she had lived more turns than Isála, she didn't wear them on her face.

This woman was not Isála's enemy.

Isála studied the young woman through the brush. What else could her hands be used for? The Mother needed more than warriors. She needed farmers, woodworkers, and artists.

The hunting party continued southwest as they passed by the hill where Isála and the siblings watched.

Her whole life, Isála had traveled the war-ridden countryside. It carried an inherent danger, but the clan had shielded her. None of the nations had a reason to attack the clan before.

However, the warriors at the lodestone had meant to kill her. Just like the hunting party vanishing into the forest meant to kill her.

For what? For orders?

The nations had effectively reached a stalemate for the past fifty turns. They wrestled disputed territories from each other like children bickering over a rag doll. Maps changed back and forth, and the only thing they had accomplished was bloodshed.

"They are heading towards the lodestone," Teshun said. "Do you think Nobel talked?"

"When I told you Nobel wouldn't talk, did I seem unsure?" Rione asked with a knife in her voice.

"Either way, General Kaiut isn't going to make this easy." He stared after the warriors, even as they had faded from view.

"When has this ever been easy, Tesh?"

"We'll have to find a place to hold up for the night soon," he said, as if there were no more conversation to be had. Then he extricated himself from the brush and made his way down the sloping hill.

Rione followed close behind, but Isála kept her distance. Her mind refused to let go of the pretty Tomakan warrior. If the General trusted her enough with a mission like this, she had probably killed before—proven herself in battle. Her hands had known blood.

It was odd to think that if Mātan hadn't taken Isála in, she could have ended up in the same position as she found herself in now—on opposite sides of a conflict with the young warrior who had passed by. The circumstances would have been different, but a strange pull of the spirits brought them together, regardless of past decisions.

Eventually, Teshun and Rione stopped in the crook of adjoining hills. The earth dancer set his things down and shifted his stance.

With one jagged movement after another, he pulled on The Mountain. A small section of clover-covered dirt shifted. The earth bent in on itself, forming a cavity in the shadowed face of the hill.

Light died beyond the small opening. Dirt compacted into solid walls, forming a small chamber barely large enough for the three of them.

Had they more time, they could have taken a longer route and kept to the denser forest. Sadly, time did not bend itself to their needs. So they followed the hills north, even as the forest grew more sparse, giving way to grasslands and further exposing them to the many searching eyes.

"It will be safe. This isn't the first time we've slept in a hole," Teshun said.

"You could have made it bigger though," Rione said.

"Do you want the patrols to find us?" Teshun spun around, facing his sister like a prairie dog challenging a mountain lion.

"It's perfect," Isála said, smiling as she looked at their tight-fitting quarters.

Amongst the promised violence, this hole in the earth served as a necessary reminder that the spirits weren't meant to be weapons. This small shelter, this gift from The Mountain, this hallow, was meant to protect.

The moons, Kana and Toka, crested towards the apex of the sky while Isála took the first watch. The long hours gave her too much time to think.

With every step north, her mother became an increasingly intrusive presence in her mind.

The River sang a gentle melody, and she wondered if her mother heard their ancestor spirit the same way. Subtle movements of The Song shifted through the trees like the curve of a riverbank.

From everything Mátan and the elders taught her about The Song, no one could predict how it would manifest itself. It took on different tones and rhythms, conjuring moods and memories, all without seeming design.

So, if her mother were listening, she and Isála would likely be hearing different aspects of The River.

"Are you paying attention?" Rione asked, as she crawled to the lip of the hallow.

"You know that my mother is the general we are on our way to see, right?"

"That isn't how questions work."

"No. You ask questions like you want to pick a fight," Isála said. "I chose to ignore it."

"Sometimes I like you, water dancer." Rione smiled and sat beside her. "If you're doing this to prove something to or about your mother, that's a shitty reason to risk your life."

"I believe in this peace as much as..."

"Settle down. I know you believe in what we're doing. You'd be denser than a fucking stone if you came out here without a bit of belief." Rione leaned back, and the moonlight caught her face as she looked up. "But we all have something driving us. Something—behind the belief."

Rione's onyx blades rested beside her.

"Do you think we'll ever know something that the wars haven't touched? Ever have a connection with someone without the weight of it being there?" Isála asked. "I never knew my mother. My father raised my brother and I while she was off fighting. So, I guess, part of me is hoping to find out who she is."

The story of how she had come to be a nomad rested in the words she hadn't said. It was common enough. One nation raided a village near a border. Whoever survived found a way to move on. Only, Isála had been four and her mother hadn't known anything about being a parent.

"Before you get to meet your mother, we are going to find ourselves in a fight, and you are going to have to decide," Rione said, her voice strangely neutral. "You may not be able to both safeguard your principles and finish what we started."

"Why is Kaiut trying so hard to stop us?"

"That's easy. It's the same reason all the other warriors keep fighting, even after everything they've lost. People fight to keep what they know because what they don't know is far scarier. If they decide not to spill blood for those stolen from them. If they put down the blades they were raised with, what will they do with their lives?"

"You're much wiser than you look," Isála said, unable to keep from grinning.

Rione pushed the younger nomad playfully. "I know. But don't let yourself think you're more enlightened than those warriors. Not when you're spouting that clan dogma like you do. You're fighting just as hard not to change."

A chill colder than the night air filled the pit of her stomach.

"You need to get some rest," Rione said before Isála could think of a response. "We have another long day of walking ahead of us."

After several breaths, Isála still had no words. She gathered her staff off the ground and crawled into the hallow, her thoughts far heavier than her bit of stormwood.

Chapter Seven

Laiken

Beliefs can be corrupted because beliefs are the teachings of the living. Beliefs are our interpretations of the spirits who exist beyond our grasp. The Mother is the land beneath our feet. She gave life to The Great Spirits, The Daughters of the sky, and even us feeble people. She didn't tell any of us why.

Still, she cared enough to gift dancers a glimpse into The Mist. The Great Spirits guide us, protect us, teach us forgiveness. How could that Mother ask us to spill blood in her name? That, I do not believe.

The Nature of The Waking, Clan Elder Tomin

Lantern light flickered over the map as Laiken traced his fingers along the aged parchment, lingering on the lodestone where the scouts had discovered his compatriots' graves.

More blood. Always more blood, he thought.

He had ordered the others to leave him alone with his thoughts. While the scouting parties scoured for the wayward envoys, he lamented over a fucking map in his tent.

Tantin had a new baby girl waiting for him back in Colian. Another child of Tomak who would never know her father's face.

What happens to a country of orphans? Who raises them to know the battles their parents fought in their names?

The night they had come upon Nobel just south of Colian, Laiken had ordered his warriors to follow the runaway nomad. Tantin and the others obeyed without question. Now, they had joined the spirits.

He had grown up with Tantin, training with The Flame, learning to serve their nation. There was not enough time to tally how often his friend had been the person he relied on.

Behind the darkness of his eyelids, he watched Tantin rush into the forest on his orders again and again.

The Song raged. The waiting heat of the world boiled beneath the surface, goading him to call on it. It hungered. It understood the need to show strength and protect one's people.

People spoke of the clan as though the nomads prized peace over all. As if the deserters followed The Mother. As if tradition meant nothing.

Blood for blood. The saying had lasted the turns for a reason.

The Mother gave The Waking to those strong enough to defend her. To honor her. Her lands and her people. Kin and country mattered. The ways of the past mattered, even if some people couldn't stomach the truth anymore.

Laiken traced the tip of his dagger through the open space between the lodestone and the Strait of Talmo.

The envoys could take thousands of paths, and Laiken only had a handful of warriors to stop them. Their future—Tomak's future—rested in the hands of twenty warriors.

The night Laiken left in search of the nomads, his father had pulled him aside.

His father, the general of the eastern front for nearly two dozen turns, wore his age heavy. White hair interlaced his naturally gray braids. Yet, he still carried himself as a warrior should—back straight, chest out, sword hung from his hip.

"Look out there," Kaiut had said, pointing to the field of waiting warriors outside of his command tent. "Twenty warriors. I am giving you command of twenty warriors. And not some pissants who haven't felt the heat of their enemy's blood on their skin. You know what those warriors could do on the frontlines."

Laiken had chosen every warrior with care. He knew very well what each of them were capable of. But his father liked to make his points, and so, Laiken didn't remind him of that fact.

"I point this out to you because I need you to understand the gravity of this mission. If you fail, we fail. The lighthearted elders in the west will go to the peace talks, and they'll make promises on behalf of our people. Promises that won't be honored. Not for long.

"And that entitled prick, Elder Grine, will force our hands. He values trade between the nations more than our safety. We will abandon our posts, and Tomakans will die. Because no matter what those bastards agree to, their political ends won't vanish because of some words scribbled on a treaty. Someone will break the accord, and we won't be prepared to stop them."

Kaiut closed the already small gap between Laiken and him before placing a hand on Laiken's shoulder. "That will not do. If you fail, *do not bother returning.* My legacy will not be carried on in a son that would fail his people."

Over the turns, Kaiut had always been a hard man with exacting standards, but he had never spoken like this before. The ever-present fire in Laiken's chest sputtered at his father's words.

"Do you understand me?"

"Yes, Father," Laiken had said, being the forever dutiful son. The words had felt like a goodbye, not because he intended to fail, but because the part of him that had always believed his father loved him past the reach of his sword had been proven wrong.

As Laiken stabbed the map with all his might, the table shuddered. His dagger stood upright, blade firmly anchored in the open lands between the end of the Kenke Forest and the sloping hills to the west of Colian.

Somewhere in that nothingness, he would find the envoys and give their blood to The Mother. For Tantin and every other Tomakan who deserved the chance to balance the blood.

He would be his father's legacy.

The furs covering the tent's entrance flapped open, and Laiken's closest living confidant, Lon, strode into the tent. A few unwieldy braids fell over her eyes, creating a shadow shifting over her cedar skin with the lantern light.

As Laiken took in the look on his friend's face, The Flame's melody settled into the sharpest edge of a blade, waiting to strike.

"You've found them?" Laiken asked, keeping the hope from his voice as much as possible. As his father said, hope is a weak warrior's excuse. True warriors had intention.

"Not quite, but something close." Lon approached the map and ripped Laiken's dagger from the table. "Here and here. Our scouts found loose soil at the bases of these hills. Freshly covered holes, easily overlooked, big enough for a few people to pass the night."

"That's all you have?"

"They covered their tracks well," Lon said, ignoring the question. "But once our scouts understood what they had found, their tracks weren't difficult to follow."

Lon drew the dagger along a path, riding the western shade of the hills.

"You ordered me to bring you whatever sign we could find of the nomads. The envoys were there."

He had thought they would have kept to the forest as long as they could. No wonder he hadn't found them.

If the nomads kept pace, they would be a day of hard travel to the north. Laiken could bring the deserting bastards to his father. Or he could always break the weak-willed envoys himself. If he discovered the location of the peace talks, they could set their enemy's war efforts back decades in a single day.

"Why are we doing this?" Lon asked.

Laiken snapped up and stared at his old friend as if a stranger had taken her place.

"What are you talking about?"

"This war took my sister just as it took your mother and brother," she said. "While it rages, I will continue to fight. I will shed blood to safekeep what is ours. But what if there is a chance for it to end? What if we can keep everyone safe without more bloodshed?"

The Flame swelled like a rush of beating drums, converging from every direction. The world beyond The Song fell silent.

Without thinking, Laiken rounded the table, grabbed Lon by the throat, and wrenched the knife from her grip. Her eyes sprang wide with the suddenness of his actions. She grabbed the hand around her throat, but he only tightened his grip.

"Have you lost your edge?" Laiken asked, spittle spraying with his consonants. "Are you shortsighted enough to think that the people who killed our families would lay down their arms because of some talks?"

Laiken brought the tip of his dagger to her throat and held it there, dimpling her skin. He had seen his father do the same to weak-willed warriors before.

Two of Laiken's warriors burst into the tent, weapons drawn. They wore the expressions of uninvited guests witnessing a moment of intimacy. And what could have been more intimate than one friend squeezing the life out of another?

With a flick of his blade in their direction, Laiken leveled his rage at the interrupting warriors. "Leave!"

The two men hesitated, exchanging a quick glance before stepping out the way they had come.

Once again alone, Laiken slid his hand from Lon's throat to the nape of her neck and settled his blade under her chin.

To her credit, Lon never made a move towards her axe or knife, both of which hung from her belt.

"Tell me once and don't lie." Laiken heard the low growl of his father's voice coming from his throat. It made him pause. He had been so much more like his mother as a boy.

But this was the way to fight a war, even if it wasn't pretty.

"Are you willing to give your blood to end this war?" he asked. "The blood of thousands of Tomakans feed The Mother's soil. Your sister's blood. My mother's and my brother's blood. Tantin's blood. Would you let their killers continue to breathe?"

She started to speak in a raspy tone, but he squeezed the back of her neck to stop her.

"Before you speak, know this. If we do not stop the nomads, our lives are forfeit. If your spirit isn't in this, tell me now and we will walk into The Mist together—get it over with. I will take your life, and I will go back to my father and offer him mine. My love for you and our bond is that strong. Family knows it is," Laiken said. "So I ask you one more time. Would you give our blood for a chance to end this war?"

As Lon swallowed, her neck caught the edge of Laiken's dagger. "No, Commander," she said, voice raw and breaking, her eyes never leaving Laiken's.

"We can never question our path. My father wouldn't have it of me, and I won't have it of you." He lowered the blade and slid it into the sheath on his hip. "The moment we waiver is the moment we die, even if it takes time for the blade to catch up."

Lon nodded, trembling as she did.

With the tenderness of their long friendship, Laiken pressed his fingers to the small cut where his knife nicked her. He offered her a slight smile. "We have too much distance to cover to linger here. Leave two warriors to break camp. They can follow once they've set the land to right and stored the supplies."

Once he released her, Lon made to leave the tent without another word.

"Lon, you know I do this for our people. We have a duty. Family knows."

"Family knows," she said, repeating the old adage without facing him.

When the furs closed over the tent's opening, Laiken looked to the flickering light. The Song wavered like the weakening flame within a dying lantern. His hands shook.

His father's hands wouldn't be shaking.

Tomak needed Laiken to be stronger. His father wouldn't live forever, and someone needed to be Tomak's spear once he crossed through to The Mist.

CHAPTER EIGHT

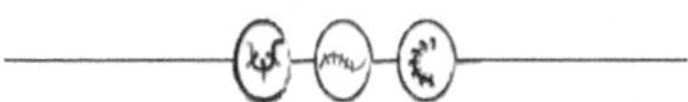

Astile once existed as a much larger nation. At the time, Tomak and Sonacoa faced continuous land disputes. Warriors on both sides of the border engaged in aggression, but it could hardly be called a war by today's standards.

Scholars have pointed to many causes for the generations of war that have ravaged Ennea, but few stand out as much as the brutal way Astile swept over the western borders of Tomak. They destroyed villages, leaving no survivors. When Tomak responded to the act of aggression, they refused to stop until Astile had shrunk to three-quarters of its original land mass.

Tomak may not have stopped their expansion into Astile if not for the war that erupted on their southern border. The treaty signed between Astile and Tomak lasted less than a decade before the conflict reignited.

Generations of War, Sonacoan Historian Katil

From the height of the hill, the fading sunlight shimmered off distant waters. Isála had not been this close to Renéqua since she was four turns. Everything about the island beyond the Strait of Talmo felt like a dream. In fact, given her age at the time, most of what she recalled probably had been a dream.

By the following night, they would cross the water.

Maybe she would instinctually know her mother. The turns of separation would vanish, and her mother's face would be as familiar as Mátan's. Older and more wrinkled, but her mother's face would fill in the memories it had abandoned.

But it had been twenty-three turns. Even if she recognized her mother, her mother would never recognize her.

"Come on, Isa. We have a good two more hours of traveling before the younger Daughters take the sky," Teshun said.

"Do you think she'll listen?" Isála asked as she descended the hill towards the siblings.

"Who?" Rione looked perturbed by the question, as if Isála had interrupted her silence.

"The girl's mother, you dolt. If you weren't my sister, I would question your parentage," Teshun said.

"The girl should be clearer. Words exist for a reason. If she means her mother, she should say so."

Teshun waved off his sister and turned his attention to Isála. "Can't say. This isn't the first time the clan has parlayed with your mother. Things must have gone well enough for them to send an invitation to the conclave."

"Same could be said for Elder Sooni. Ask Nobel how that turned out," Rione said.

"You think Isála's mother is going to butcher us like Kaiut? We have the best protection there is—a mother's love." Teshun made an exaggerated gesture to his heart.

"More like a mother's guilt," Isála said.

"As long as I don't get porcupined with arrows, I'll take it," Rione said.

"You really can be a cruel bitch, you know that?" Teshun pushed his sister, though she didn't budge from her path.

The two continued to bicker, and Isála drifted behind them, lost in her thoughts.

All the conjecture in the world wouldn't matter in a day. When they arrived on the shore of Renêqua, the black flag would either be honored or not. Her mother would either remember her or not. Renêqua would either join the conclave, or the wars would continue to rage on.

"Shut your face," Teshun hissed, as he knelt and placed his hand to the ground.

Rione pulled her onyx axes from their cradles and shrank into a battle-ready stance.

"We need to move." Teshun darted to the west without another word.

For all Rione's hubris, she didn't hesitate to follow her brother. She knew his gift. When he heard trouble rumbling through The Song, she didn't doubt him and neither would Isála.

Her feet scrambling to keep up with the siblings, Isála searched for a sign of the enemy. Nothing. Not a noise. Not a shadow. Only the knowledge that every stride took her farther from the answers which lay on the other side of the Strait of Talmo.

Isála recalled the fear she had felt beside the lodestone with each breath. Each footfall reverberated through her body. Her stormwood staff grew heavier, and the night went silent beneath the rushing torrent of The River's call.

A blotch of red uniforms crested the hill behind her, cloaked by dusk and distance.

An arrow sank into the earth to her right. Another veered off somewhere in the darkening landscape.

As sporadic and ill-aimed as the arrows were, one lucky bolt could end a life as easily is a well-aimed one.

The ironoaks head promised safety of a sort, but it wouldn't be enough.

The Strait of Talmo was still a day to the north.

They had found them. There were too many to fight. She had failed.

If the warriors got too close, Isála would have to destroy the letter before they could take it. Even if it meant an end to the conclave and an end to her too short time in The Waking, she couldn't let Kaiut discover where the peace talks would be held.

"Hey, water dancer, how about a little cover?" Rione yelled over her shoulder without slowing pace.

Her voice echoed in Isála's head as she tried to decipher the words. Nothing made sense besides running.

Another volley of arrows crashed into the dirt behind them.

"Now, Isála. Right fucking now!"

The Song shook like a storm, cracking and rumbling through her. Then a separate, unassuming chorus hummed within the tumultuous overtones. It moved as if the chaos of the world would not bother it from its path.

This second soft force called to her, and she danced.

Even as her feet continued to race behind the siblings, her hands plucked at the wavelength surrounding her, pulling at the water clinging to the air. Vapor cooled and thickened. She fed the fog her breath, and it swelled to encompass them.

As they filtered through the gaps in the tree line, the forest canopy shrouded them from the last of Sokan's light.

Rione grabbed Isála. "You need to be in this. This is the time where all that talk of ending the war ceases to be talk."

"Are we going to die?" Isála hated the sound of her voice as it left her mouth.

"We are going to fight." Rione shook Isála as she spoke.

"We can't," Isála said. "There are too many of them."

"The strait is too far away, and if we don't make it across the water in the next two days, this is all for nothing," Teshun said, his voice finding a calm that it had no right to. "We need to move now. We pick our ground, and we hold it."

———————

Laiken led seven of his warriors through the fog at a crawl, a sword in each hand. The others would be patrolling the Tomakan side of the strait should he fail.

No matter how well-tested his warriors were, these envoys had killed three blooded Tomakans at the lodestone. They managed to escape a potential ambush, and they had at least one dancer amongst them.

Fools who underestimated their enemies died foolish deaths.

He motioned for his warriors to stow their bows and spread as the forest snuffed out the sky's light.

"Lon, Yille, and Ettena, come with me. The rest of you ride our flank to the west. Take your time. Watch your backs. But, above all, get me that letter," Laiken said. "You fail me, you fail my father and you fail Tomak. Now go."

The closeness of his father's words to his own gave him a moment's pause. Do not bother returning. The words became an echo in his head.

Laiken's father had always said he was too much like his mother—too soft. The General had found ways to toughen him up, especially after his brother died. He never wanted to be like his father, but maybe Tomak needed him to be.

Some moments trapped too much meaning within them. If Laiken didn't fuck this up, he and his father would advance the Tomakan war effort further an anyone in the history of their nation.

If he failed, he would lose his father in a far different way than he had lost his mother.

The forest floor rose gently as they walked north. Ironoak trees shielded everything from view in the near-absolute shade of the canopy.

The Flame kindled within the heart of every tree, ready to consume. It thrummed with yearning, the pace burgeoning as he crept further into the forest.

Some people became anxious before battle. Not Laiken. The same anticipation that wove through The Song called him to rush forward. He had to restrain himself lest he get too excited.

These nomads would be worthy kills.

A massive shadow shifted, and a pair of black-as-night axes crashed into Ettena, lifting her from her feet. As soon as his compatriot crashed to the forest floor, the nomad wrenched an axe free and buried the blade in Ettena's face for good measure.

Worthy kills, he thought as he let The Song loose.

The bark of several nearby trees heated as he swept his arms forward, then they erupted into flames.

He couldn't help but smile at the large nomad with bloody black axes.

CHAPTER NINE

Peace is a fragile thing. Even in the smallest of communities, life challenges peace on a daily basis. We may not be working towards peace right now. Maybe we are only working towards ending the bloodshed. We can work for peace afterwards.

Excerpt from a transcribed conversation between Clan elders Tomin and Yuei

The plan had been simple. At least it had sounded simple to Isála when Teshun and Rione explained it. They found the most defensible position they could in the forest, with the slope of the land on their side. Rione would attack first. Teshun would cover her with throwing knives from behind a rock formation, and Isála would engage any stray fighters.

They had spoken about it as if it were commonplace. Then the planning was over, replaced by a haunting silence.

In the few moments before the warriors found them, Isála took the letter from her bag and buried it at the base of a tree. She covered the leather pouch and etched a marker in the tree with the solemnity of burying a loved one. Then she waited, gripping her staff as if she could crush the nearly indestructible wood.

If not for the promise of death, this situation would have been laughable.

The nations had fought each other for nearly a century over lines drawn on a map, resources, and a few powerful people's desire for more. The fighting never did anything for the average Ennean. Yet, these warriors coming to kill them had dedicated themselves so deeply to the idea of blood for blood that they would kill to avoid peace.

No one had to die. Every act of violence required a choice.

Isála rested her shoulder against a tree as she searched the forest for their attackers. She had seen countless nights like this. The forest slept beneath the younger Daughters, small noises only accentuating the silence. And for all its normalcy, it may have been her last night in The Waking.

Nothing and nobody moved until Rione rounded the tree and crashed into the first warrior coming up the hill.

Pops of yellow and orange flashed overhead, then flames grabbed hold of the tree limbs. The fires rushed from tree to tree, consuming everything, including the darkness. A warrior brandishing two swords rose his arms with a flourish, and the blaze grew brighter.

Isála froze, watching as if an observer in a stranger's nightmare. Rione wrenched her axes from a dead woman's chest and skull before slamming into the fire dancer.

But he did not fall so easily. The fire dancer's twin swords rose to meet every strike Rione executed.

The ravenous warriors rounded each other, onyx clashing with steel in a cacophony of sharp clangs. Flickering light contorted the scene as if their movements jumped from one fixed moment of entangled weapons to the next. Neither backed down. Neither found openings in the other's defenses. Both smiled as they chased each other's blood.

And Isála could do nothing.

Two other warriors took shelter behind ironoaks as Teshun flung his onyx knifes from behind the relative safety of his cluster of jagged rocks. Eventually, he would run out of knives. The only question was if the other warriors would be breathing when he did.

But as she watched, that was not what most concerned Isála.

In the chaos of their escape, she hadn't been able to count the red robes in pursuit. Still, the mass of warriors who had chased them into the forest had certainly been larger than four.

Before she escaped too deep into her worries, one of the warriors pinned down by Teshun's throwing knives disappeared into a cloud of shadows.

It had been foolish of her to think, even for a second, that they hadn't brought more than one dancer. Her fear and her stupidity would get her killed, and worse, the peace the Clan had labored so hard to create would die beside her.

A branch eaten away by the flames above crashed to the ground and woke Isála from her self-pity. Its light caught a shadow that didn't bend in its presence, and she darted towards the anomaly before she could think better of it.

The River screamed with the force of a careening waterfall.

The shadow-cloaked figure raced towards Teshun, but Isála found it first. She lunged into a blot of darkness thicker than the night surrounding it, finding flesh and cloth. Staff in hand, she grasped bits of clothing and limbs as her momentum threw her down the hill.

———

Teshun looked at the spot where that foolish girl crashed into a shadow, as if the darkness had done her wrong. Even more ridiculously, she had managed to grasp the shadows.

As Isála and the shadow dancer he hadn't seen toppled down the hill, Teshun's fear went with them. Whether or not he could explain what he had seen made no difference. It was objectively funny to see someone wrestle with shadows.

From around an ironoak, a Tomakan warrior stared at the same spot, sporting a gape-mouthed expression.

Whatever animus might exist between them, Teshun and his attacker shared far more than he would care to admit. The man looked as if he could be a cousin. With that busted nose, maybe a distant cousin. But a cousin, nonetheless.

"Fucking funny, right?" Teshun shouted before whipping a knife at his target. It clattered against a tree as the man tucked behind his cover.

As the fires overhead grew, smoke filled the air and ash fluttered down.

This standoff couldn't last forever. As he rifled through the leather pouch at his waist, his fingers counted five more knives.

He and his sister had escaped far too many dangerous situations in the past. The Mist must have been expecting them by now.

Glimpses of Rione raging against the fire dancer flittered through the gaps in the forest. There weren't many who could hold his sister back, but the dual-sword wielding bastard seemed to have kept his blood in his skin sack fairly well.

Maybe they would finally be off to see their mother.

The Mountain sang a steady song—the sort of solid rhythm people expected of stone. But she had the ability to shift like rivers, to flare with pressure, to sink and bellow.

Crouching behind the rock formation, he stared at the patch of earth beneath his busted-nose accoster. The soil had been well fed with rainwater, clinging tightly to itself. The deeper The Song pierced the earth, the more stones lined the dirt until ever-larger rock slabs fused into the foundation of the forest. Pressure pounded through The Song like a needy pulse.

Teshun spread his legs, anchoring his feet firmly in the dirt. He reached his hand beyond the bounds of his stone protection, towards the ground beneath his enemy's feet.

Deep within the earth, Teshun felt the stone shift with him. Then everything flashed white.

An arrow sank deep into his palm, the force twisting him from his anchored position. He crumpled to the ground, as more arrows tinked against the stone.

Looking at the shaft of wood protruding from either side of his hand, it seemed an oddity at first. This wasn't where an arrow belonged. Then pain ripped through his body like lightning, jolting outward from the point of impact.

His fatalistic thoughts of crossing into The Mist with Rione twisted into bitter anger. He and his sister had done nothing but try to save these blood-guzzling, broken-spirit assholes from their awful fucking selves. Maybe they had the right idea. Maybe it would be best to send his enemies into The Mist.

Four archers crept up the hill with their aim searching for a clear view of him. Any one of them could have released the arrow embedded in his hand, but they all would face the same consequences.

The pulse of pressure beneath them swelled with Teshun's rage.

Let them die in The Mother's embrace, he thought.

———

The fire dancing prick smiled as Rione pressed her attack. His twin swords angled this way and that as if he could predict where she would strike next. Still, she persisted.

If she allowed him a moment to bring The Flame into their fight, none of the nomads would survive the night.

Smoke filled the forest, limiting her view beyond a few paces and shrinking the world to the intimacy of this singular fight. The rising heat and the consequences of every action were merely a stage for their battle.

Reaching an axe forward like a hook, she caught the hilt of his sword with the curve of her weapon. But before she could make use of the hold, he forced her back with a well-timed thrust of his second sword, smiling at the small cut she left on his hand.

The pair of them could be fighting till sunrise, which would not do. Tesh needed her. The stuck-up water dancer needed her too, though that was less urgent.

A branch cracked above them before crashing down a few paces off in a spray of sparks. The burning branch lit his face at a new angle. Beyond his smile, some deeper need pushed through—the look of a warrior who chose the fight for reasons other than survival or simple rage. This man had something to prove. He would not yield until her axe opened him up.

"You're willing to burn your nation to the ground to stop us? Seems counter-intuitive." Rione leveled a heavy overhead strike towards his clavicle, stopped by a well-positioned deflection.

"Don't worry," the fire dancer said. "I'll put out the flames before we bury you."

His left blade feigned a cross-body attack only for him to sweep his right at her forward leg. The hot pain of the metal slicing into her calf only drove her into a deeper rage. It would take far more than a scratch to deter her.

Another branch fell behind her.

"I'm going to enjoy bleeding you." Her axes came down with such force that his feet slipped as he blocked the attack with both of his blades.

———

Isála tumbled to a stop at the bottom of the hill several paces away from the shadow dancer. Fear and trepidation heightened the dim world around them. She scrambled to her feet, collecting her staff from the dirt before the Tomakan woman could shelter herself in shadows once again.

Perhaps sensing Isála wouldn't give her the opportunity to pull on her spirit ancestor, the woman jumped to her feet with her hand axe and long knife readied.

"Fucking Nomad. You'll be more use when the buzzards are picking over your rotting corpse." The warrior bared her teeth in a snarl.

Despite the fear coursing through Isála's body, her training took hold. The countless hours of sparring with Mátan had seeped into her muscles. She swept her staff at her opponent's legs to keep her from finding balance before attacking with a series of strikes aimed at her chest and arms.

The longer she could keep her opponent off-balance, the greater her chances of surviving.

The warrior stumbled back to dodge the flurry of blows, raising her blades to deflect what she couldn't avoid. Her snarl twisted into confusion, as if she couldn't have imagined Isála would be anything but a clumsy little girl.

Catching the stormwood staff with her axe, the warrior lashed out, swiping her blade at Isála's gut. But the movement was too slow. Isála hadn't allowed the shadow dancer to find proper footing.

As her uncle taught her, a fight began and ended with one's stance.

Isála's staff found flesh, crashing into the woman's shoulder. Every third strike or so, she was able to find a gap in the warrior's defenses.

"Dancers rely too much on what makes them powerful," Mátan had constantly said during their training. "They forget the spirits aren't weapons and neglect their true weapons."

Shadow dancers had a reputation for leaping out from the shadows for a quick kill—strategic engagements rather than direct combat. No matter how many people this dancer had spirited on, she hadn't the skills for a single dual without her spirit to hide her.

The warrior slipped a foot through the dirt, expanding her stance, and swept her blades wide. As her knife hand remained steady, she bounced the other to a silent rhythm. Shadows flowed away from the point under her axe, leaving only the light from the distant fires to fill the void.

Shadow dancer tricks, Isála thought before slamming her staff down on the woman's wrist. A pop and a scream cracked the quiet between them, her wrist bending at an unnatural angle.

Independent strands of shade slithered back into place as the shadow dancer cradled her injury.

This violence could allow Isála to continue her mission. It could end the war, and it didn't require killing a fellow child of Ennea.

Isála rotated the staff and knocked the warrior prone. With her weapon raised to the sky, she struck towards her opponent's face, only to halt a breath away from contact.

"Yield," she said. "This doesn't have to be."

Faster than any previous movement, the shadow dancer plucked her axe from the ground, hooking Isála's foot in the process.

The world twisted, and the ground became the sky as Isála landed flat on her back. Her breath and staff escaped her the instant she landed, the force quaking through her spine.

True to a warrior's nature, the shadow dancer didn't hesitate to attack with a killing strike. Except, her axe found Isála's outstretched hand.

Blood and pain came in equal measure as Isála stared at the space where part of her palm and her two smallest fingers had been. Screams rolled out of her of their own volition, filling her eardrums.

The shape of her hand ended so bluntly. It hadn't looked like that a moment ago. Blood welled, darkening her skin in the firelight.

The warrior readjusted, careful of her limp arm—bones loose under her flesh. She raised the axe above her head.

This was it—the moment of Isála's failure.

The numb feeling that had cradled her pain erupted into an angry storm of violence. The tumult of agony unleashed every clashing emotion of abandonment, rage, frustration, hopelessness.

She had only wanted to protect people. Show them they could live without this chaos. She had meant to succeed her way. She had meant to be better than her mother. Everything she had been through to become the person she intended to be fractured in the instant she plunged her uncle's knife into the shadow dancer's neck.

Time stopped, and her attacker's expression slackened. The angle of her brow, which had been so sharp, drooped. The harsh line of her lips fell agape. She looked helpless.

The woman's blood flowed warm over Isála's skin, tickling the hairs on her arm. She held the knife in place. If she moved, the woman would fall.

Jolts of pain started the flow of time once again. Her wound itched and burned along the cut before an unbearable strain tore up the length of her arm.

Despite her fevered agony, she lifted her bloody hand to the other side of the shadow dancer's neck. Her blood coated the woman's skin and robes as she lowered her enemy to Ennea's blessed body.

Isāla stared down at her hand still clutching the hilt of her uncle's knife. Blood ran slick over the metal. The blade ended abruptly as it pierced the shadow dancer's flesh. She let it go and threw herself away from the body, crawling backwards through the dirt.

"What have I done?"

Every principle Isāla carried like a scared flame fizzled out alongside the light in the shadow dancer's eyes. With it, her anger broke. Her hand throbbed, a perpetual sensation of teeth digging into her flesh. It felt deserved.

"I'm sorry," she said. "Blessed Mother, I'm sorry."

Teshun planted his injured hand against the rock formation with the arrow resting against the flattest surface he could find. Free hand wrapped around the fletching, he snapped the shaft. The world flashed white. Pain cracked his spirit in unison with the splintering wood, but he didn't have the time to moan about discomfort as long as he remained on this side of The Mist.

The Mountain bellowed along with his pain. The melodies within The Song crashed into one another. Then he focused on the approaching archers, and The Song settled into a singular chorus.

These four red-robed bastards were a waste of their fathers' seed. They stalked up the slope like hunters, not understanding what happened when they cornered dangerous prey.

As Teshun danced, he twisted the pressure within the earth at the base of the hill. The foundation beneath the surface shifted, and his body shifted with it.

An arrow clanged against the rock formation, but he didn't move from the safety of his cover.

At first, the ground created a small divot at the base of the hill. Nothing that anyone would notice. But below the surface, gaps opened. Pockets of empty space craved fulfillment. Soil shifted under the warriors' feet. Then, as the balance holding everything in place shattered, the hill turned into a river of dirt.

The four archers scrambled to find safe footing, but there was none to be had. They clambered, reaching out wildly, trying to stay above the surface. One archer's leg got stuck in the roaring rapids of shifting earth before he sank into its downward flow. He screamed. Then the others followed suit.

Their bodies tumbled in the landslide. They crawled towards the air, only to be pulled down deeper.

Teshun continued to dance, his arms twisting apart and creating more pressure filled gaps in the earth below his enemies.

Then the screaming stopped.

The Mother could sort them out and bring them to The Mist.

Trembling coursed through Teshun's body as he stopped pulling at his connection to The Mountain. His anger abandoned him and exhaustion settled into his bones.

When he turned his attention back to the warrior who had been hiding behind the ironoaks, old busted nose was charging towards him. The man raged in a noiseless scream as he careened towards the rock formation.

Teshun fumbled through his knife pouch and flung an onyx blade at the bastard. It sank into his shoulder, but didn't stop his momentum. As Teshun reached for another, the warrior leaped over the rocks, blade readied.

The handle of a throwing knife found Teshun's good hand just before the warrior crashed into him.

They collapsed to the dirt, heavy unmoving bodies.

Teshun's stomach felt warm as blood saturated his robes.

The warrior's eyes lost focus, then rolled back.

Teshun had been right. This close—the warrior really could have been kin. The shape of their faces, the cut of their brow. They could have been so much more than enemies.

Teshun rolled the other man off himself, then tried to get up. But as he rose, the sword buried in his gut pulled against the movement.

It didn't hurt. It felt like a pressure pulling at the slightest motion—the slightest breath.

Everything wavered, and his head fell back to the ground.

———

Tendons in Rione's shoulders strained as she continued to bombard the fire dancer with one strike after another. The one time she let him create a distance in the fight, he began dancing and nearly set her robes aflame.

The ever-increasing smoke made each breath less fulfilling than the last. Heat lapped against her, but it only managed to make her more aware of the way her body moved.

With every flicker of the flames, the light cut his face at a different angle, and she found something new to hate about the smug Tomakan. The shadow undercut his deep brown eyes, making him all-too-human.

All Isāla's fucking whining about the value of a life flittered through Rione's head.

Of course, lives had value, which was why pricks like this had to die. How many more would live out their turns in The Waking if only he were buried deep in The Mother's waiting grasp?

She hooked one of his swords in the crook of her axe blade for the dozenth time, but he pushed the blade deeper and withdrew it in a swift motion, drawing another shallow cut along her arm.

Each of the several cuts stung when she moved. The pain blended into one sharp spark that traveled across her body.

She wouldn't last like this. He had drawn far more blood than she had.

"You getting winded, nomad?"

Rione slammed her midnight blade into the cross-catch of his two swords. "Let's see if you die with that smile."

Ash showered down as a branch cracked overhead before falling next to them and forcing them to maneuver to the side.

"The forest can burn down around us, and I will still be standing, ready to bury my axes in your dense skull," Rione said.

"When I started my hunt, I never imagined I would find such a worthy opponent." The fire dancer angled out from a strike and lunged forward in a too-obvious attack. "Tell me. How many warriors have you spirited on? How much blood have you claimed for peace?"

Rione swiped her blade down at his shoulder, but he caught the blade and immediately attacked with his off-hand sword. Light reflected off the metal as it shot forward over her opposite shoulder. With a simple turn of her free axe, she caught the second blade in the entangled mess of metal and onyx.

"Peace is the bloodiest word I know," she said, pushing into him as their weapons clung to each other. "But it's worth fighting for. Can you say the same of your vengeance?"

A crack broke through the sky.

They shoved off each other just before a burning branch crashed into the ground between them.

Rione fell to her knees, catching her balance, but it was already too late. The bastard had started twirling his arms like a fucking bird during mating season. The air around her shimmered with heat.

Any instant, the air would heat until the pressure exploded in a flash of fire. She had seen it countless times. The cowardice of fire dancers knew no bounds.

Maybe Isála had been right in a way. If they couldn't find a way to peace without spilling blood, maybe they didn't deserve it.

Although that probably wasn't the point the girl had intended on making.

Rione did the only thing she could to save her weary hide and threw her axe, blade over handle, through the air.

The weight had never been balanced for throwing, but if she was going to die, at least she would die fighting.

The blade caught the light and fell into the darkness with every rotation. Then the fire dancer's hands fell still.

He stared at her, flabbergasted for a moment before collapsing to the earth.

His eyelids twitched as she bent over him. He coughed, but his expression remained slack.

"You fought well for a blood-hungry bastard," she said.

"I failed him." The man's eyes shut once more, tears tracing a path from both eyes down his cheeks.

The man's ribcage clung to her axe as she yanked it from the new cavity in his chest.

When she finished with the others, she would give him a proper burial. She wiped her axe on his robes to clean away the gore.

Before she could stand, Isāla screamed.

———

Blood flowed between the fingers of Isāla's uninjured hand as she held the wound in Teshun's belly, the sword still protruding.

"Don't die. You can't die," she said. "Who's going to keep your sister and I from killing each other?"

Teshun's laugh turned into a cough, spraying bloodied spittle from his lips. "You two are more similar than you think."

His voice rang hollow, the vibrancy it had once held, filled with shallow breaths.

"Plus, I think Rione would find a bit of satisfaction if you actually tried to kill her."

A chill shuddered through her chest as she saw the shadow dancer's lifeless body behind her closed eyelids.

Rione leaped over the rock formation and froze.

"Is it that bad?" Teshun asked.

"Where were you?!" Rione yelled at Isāla. "You were supposed to have his back. Were you hiding while we fought? Were you too fucking scared of blood?"

As tears built up in Isāla's eyes, her words left her. She could only stare up at Rione.

The older nomad rushed to her brother's side and shoved Isála out of the way.

"Don't be that way, sis." He coughed, more blood reddening his lips. "The girl did good. Took on a shadow dancer."

"Why did you let this happen to you? I need you. You know that."

He reached up to grab her shoulder, but his hand slipped. She caught it and held it. "They really didn't want us to make it north, huh?" he asked.

Isála watched the woman who had been as hard as the onyx blades she carried slump into a cracked mold of herself. Rione grimaced as she cried, looking around at the sky and forest as if there were something that could save her brother.

"You have to do it, Rione. You have to finish this."

"I can't. Not without you," she said. "You have been there every single day of my life. I'm not me without you."

"You always thought fighting made you strong, but you were strong long before you held an axe. Even though you're short, I always looked up to you." He smiled with bloody lips.

"Can't you ever be serious?"

Teshun broke into a fit of coughing. "Do you think I'll find Mom on the other side?"

Rione bent her forehead to her brother's chest and cried while he patted her scarf-covered head.

"Thank you for being my sister." His voice more breath than sound.

"Thank you for..." Rione stopped as Teshun's hand slipped from its place on her head. She picked herself up, shaking her head. "No. Blessed Mother, no. Please."

Isála didn't move as Rione begged Ennea until her tears overtook her breath.

CHAPTER TEN

ISÁLA

Emotions are not an enemy to peace. Anger, bitterness, resentment—every single negative emotion is as much a part of peace as happiness and love. Only by addressing our emotions can we find a path through. Peace requires us to be who we are first. We cannot find an enemy on the inside and hope to create peace on the outside.

Understanding War, Clan Elder Sinoe

With part of her hand missing, each mound of dirt Isála ripped from the earth sent lightning through her arm. But Teshun deserved whatever peace she and Rione could give him. She dug the shadow dancer's axe deeper into the hole, shoveling away another clump of dirt.

Despite the hours that had passed and the mound of displaced earth that continued to grow, Rione hadn't said a word. She simply dug deeper.

Above them, smoke continued to rise into the night. Isála had calmed the fires with The River, but only time would temper the trees' wounds.

It had meant nothing. This destruction and death hadn't solved anything.

People died all the time. The wars stole families from The Waking one piece after another, but the grief never stopped. Just because something was inevitable didn't diminish the pain of it.

And now, Isála had become a part of the cycle in a new way. She had sent a spirit into The Mist, plunged her uncle's knife into another person's neck.

The woman's final look of surprise lingered in the forest's shadows.

People always spoke about the need to kill—the circumstances that required it, as if their justification made the life they stole less valuable.

In that moment, it had truly been Isála's life or the shadow dancer's.

Fuck, she thought. She didn't even know the woman's name.

The weighing of her life for another felt like an excuse. She had betrayed the peace she pledged herself to and become closer to her mother's daughter.

Yet, as she thrust the axe into the dirt, she wondered if she would have killed to save Teshun. If a life had to be snuffed out from existence, wouldn't it have been better for Teshun to be breathing instead of some Tomakan warrior?

Like he had said, "Inaction can kill as easily as a blade."

Tears fell anew from Isála's puffy eyes, soaking into the soil.

After the long hours of digging, then covering Teshun's lifeless body with dirt, Isála stood beside Rione. The light of The Daughters slipped through the canopy and cast a soft glow on the ground, separating the fresh grave from its surroundings with subtle incongruities.

Isála knelt beside the grave. "Blessed Mother, welcome Teshun. Offer him the peace we couldn't obtain in The Waking. We were too damn selfish and angry. To The Mountain, continue to support him in The Mist as you did in The Waking."

As she raised her hand to her lips to kiss three fingers, she stopped, looking at her maimed hand. She chuckled to herself, a bitter sound. She had always used her left hand to thank The Mother. Why should she stop now?

She kissed her thumb along with her other remaining fingers and touched them to the dirt.

"You should get some sleep." Rione's voice sounded empty. All her fight, anger, and life escaped her, leaving her words bland.

When Isála looked up towards the older woman, Rione didn't return her gaze.

"Tesh died for this," Rione said. "There is no way I am going to dishonor that. We leave with the sunrise."

The poultice covering Isála's injury itched as they walked. She wanted to rub her missing fingers against the grit of her travel sack, but she had to remind herself they weren't there.

It seemed a selfish thing to mourn the loss of a couple of fingers when her friend lay in The Mother's embrace. Then again, her mourning took on multiple facets, shifting and reforming as they walked. It became anger before self-pity. It took the shape of the shadow dancer's face and swelled into shame.

When the pain in her hand spiked, she tried to remember their mission. But that too conjured bitter thoughts of the wars that should never have been and which forced her along this path.

Walking gave her plenty of time to hover over each loss, careful to never fall in too deeply. Before she could properly mourn what she had lost, she would have to survive the coming day. Rione had been right. Teshun deserved that much.

While Isála tottered from one horrible thought to the next, Rione carried on her own vigil of silence, only breaching it to suggest they break this way or that around an obstruction in the woods.

Isála drank from her waterskin, and old passages written by clan elders echoed in her mind. She had built her understanding of the world upon texts and sayings.

Peace is not a belief. It is a practice. It is the active struggle to love the world around you and all of those who inhabit it. Elder Tomin had so many beautiful ideas, but had they ever been challenged? If Elder Tomin had been in her place, would he have let the shadow dancer kill him? With all the implications and consequences of failing to deliver their missive?

The weight of the leather pouch and its contents pulled at her travel sack as she thought about what she had done to keep it safe.

Rione walked several paces ahead of her, saying nothing. One foot in front of the other, as if nothing had changed. As if all that mattered was the next step.

"Talk!" Isála yelled. "Say something! Scream at me! He should be alive instead of me. Isn't that what you're thinking? Why is this kid who doesn't know anything about the world trudging through the forest with me instead of him?"

Rione stopped, and the quiet grew louder as she turned.

"That's not what I'm thinking at all," Rione said in a low hum of a voice. "I'm thinking that I hate that I was right. You had to choose between your principles and your life. They forced you to do that. Yeah, you were annoying before, but that was your choice. They made the choice to force you to kill, and I hate them for that.

"I hate that my brother and I are apart for the first time in our—my life. Every fucking thing that I have been through, my brother has been there, talking too much. Now, it's so damn quiet. But I have to go on. We have to go on. Because if we don't, he died for nothing."

"What comes after we deliver the message?"

Rione chuckled. "Kid, I don't think a single person in Ennea can answer that question, and you are wildly optimistic if you don't think there is another fight between us and finding out."

"We have to, right?"

"Right," Rione said. "Now, walk up here with me. You might not be him, but it would be nice to have someone where he should be. Can you do that?"

Without another word, Isála took her place beside Rione.

Sokan set. Before she rose again, they would need to be across the strait.

If they had been allowed to stick to the hills, they would have reached the shores of Renêqua by now. Instead, they had been forced to flee to the relative safety of the forest. And in a day, that safety would end, leaving them open to the world.

Whatever awaited them would likely make Isála choose her principles or her mission again.

A small part of her hoped they had built up the enemy in their minds. Maybe the hunting party that had found them had been the only remaining obstacle.

Looking at her injured hand, she knew it was a fool's hope. The missing piece of her tingled along the poultice, burning hotter the more she thought about it. And she couldn't help thinking about it.

Rione shared out a handful of saltmeat, and Isála forced herself to eat it. Even though she was full of nerves and regrets, her stomach needed the food.

"Make me a promise," Rione said, sitting with her back against an ironoak in the dark.

"I'm not going in planning to kill. I know I might have to, but I'm not after blood."

"Are you going to let me finish what I want to say, or do you already know everything I'm thinking?"

Isála waved her hand with a flourish to invite Rione to speak.

"We only have one goal tomorrow. We need to deliver you and that letter across the water. If I tell you to leave me behind, you leave me behind. Got it?"

Even without the light from a fire or one of The Daughters, Isála could read the sincerity plainly on Rione's face. A strange heat boiled in her gut.

"After everything, you are going to sacrifice yourself? Are you trying to be a martyr?"

"Listen, water dancer. This isn't about me. We have a mission, and I'm not going to fail something this important."

"I know he's dead," Isála said. "But that doesn't mean you have to run off into The Mist to find him."

"Watch it." Rione leaned forward in challenge.

"No. You're ready to die and all. Why not say the truth? You're too scared to live without him. You want to have a reason to die."

"If you don't get that message to your precious mommy, the lot of us are fucked," Rione said. "Remove your head from your perpetually clenched ass and realize this isn't about you and me."

"This has nothing to do with my mother."

"Ennea's bloody tits, it doesn't. You're on this mission because of your mother. You convinced the elders you would be the best hope to get a message to her. I didn't bring the great General into this. You did."

Isála's ears throbbed with the blood rushing through her head. She wanted to lunge at the bitter old warrior, but she wouldn't survive that encounter. And she was right.

When Isála approached the elders, she had done exactly as Rione said. The General's guilt was Isála's greatest weapon.

"Tomorrow, I am going to do everything I have to and bring this message across the strait. If I have to leave you behind, I will. If I have to use my mother's name and position, I will. But if you run towards your death like a coward, I won't pray for you. I won't tell people of your bravery. I'll do everything I can to forget you."

"You think I care?

Silence sat between them for a moment. Then Isála took a breath to settle herself. "I know you do. You want to matter to someone, and I'm all you have now."

CHAPTER ELEVEN

ISÁLA

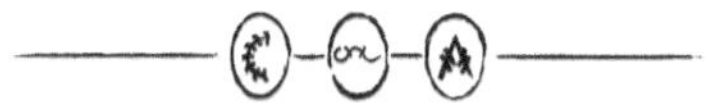

*Blood owes blood came from an Astilean phrase predating common tongue,
meaning what belongs to one belongs to their kin. Over the turns, it became a
phrase of retribution, though the impetus for the change is unclear.*

The History of Our Tongues, Astilean linguist Jonal

Within an hour, Isála could be on the shores of the homeland she couldn't
remember. However, the small fires interrupting the field of night stretching
between her and the water promised to challenge her for every step.

"We knew there would be more warriors to contend with," Rione said
from over her shoulder.

As true as that may have been, seeing the fires made taking her first step
past the tree line into flat open fields nearly impossible. People would die
tonight. Isála, maybe. Or Rione.

Or more anonymous warriors who she would forever remember.

Rione bent down and riffled through her travel sack, pulling out a
handful of supplies until she found a small, hollow length of wood. *A
whistle?*

"What are you doing?" Isála asked.

"Whether or not we make it across that field, we won't have need for any of that other shit. But this," she said, holding up the whistle. "This could mean the difference between meeting a friend or an enemy on the other side of that water."

Looking at her staff, the bit of stormwood she had carried with her since the first time she saw one of the rare black-as-night trees, she knew she couldn't take it with her. It would only slow her down, and now was not the time for sentimentality. She would have to rely on The River and the knife her uncle had given her.

She leaned it against the crook of an ironoak, her fingers lingering on the wood.

After leaving her staff behind, Isála considered abandoning the rest of her supplies with it. What would she need other than the letter? She bent down to search for anything she couldn't leave behind.

Inside the sack, she found the black flag Elder Melin had given her, a sign of peaceful passage. The silly fabric wouldn't do anything to shield them from their enemies. Yet, something about it pulled her. It symbolized what this journey was supposed to be about. A field of black—the embodiment of The Mother's soil and the night sky. That was what they fought for.

Isála removed the flag and wrapped it around her waist. "I'm ready."

A small smile tugged at Rione's lips, her eyes still red and puffy from her silent mourning. "How about it, water dancer? You think The River could give us a little help?"

Despite Isála's anxiety, The River sang like soft dew gathered before sunrise. It did not push or prod, it existed as something momentary that would become a different version of itself in the heat of the morning.

The morning could bring many things. Isála herself could be bound to the fucking spiritual plane.

She took a deep breath and let herself fall into The Song. Not so deeply she might lose herself in its wake. Only deep enough to allow The River to whisper the most minute connections to the water surrounding her.

Arms reaching towards the sky, she collected the vapor in the air. It cooled and thickened in her grasp. The sky grew darker as clouds rebuffed Kana and Toka's light. Her feet shifted with the water's desire to move, but she wouldn't allow it. Not yet.

The Song grew fuller, reflecting the controlled chaos building in the sky. The melody verged on the edge of a crescendo, threatening to crash at any moment. And still, she restrained its need.

The River—the spirit of patience—could only endure so long before it would crack. Then, at the precipice of The Song's need, Isāla broke her hold. The clouds above released their bounty, turning the night into a blur of water raging from the sky.

"That will do." Rione stepped out of the relative cover of the forest canopy and into the rain.

The fires in the distance had all gone quiet under the raging storm, which meant it would be harder for the warriors to find them, but it would also be impossible to know where the warriors might be lurking.

Especially without Teshun.

They didn't need to move fast. They had the night to find their way to the strait. So, Isāla followed Rione's lead, crouching low as they moved through the farmland.

With every step, Isāla moved closer to the mother who had abandoned her.

It was the last thing Isāla should have been worried about. She had killed for the first time. Half her hand was missing and the other half stung with varying intensity every time she moved. Teshun had died. Even now, trudging through a storm of her own design, some unknown number of warriors were actively trying to kill her. And if they succeeded, a once in a generation chance at peace would die with her. Yet, the idea of seeing her mother—a woman who might not even recognize her—loomed like a louder threat than any other.

It shouldn't have mattered.

Her mother had given her away. Isāla didn't have to forgive her or love her. All she had to do was pull on her mother's guilt enough. Earlier envoys had gotten her to the edge of agreeing to the conclave. Isála could make it happen.

Rione grabbed Isála's shoulder and gestured to the right.

The roar of the rain washed out all other sounds, but shadows cut silhouettes in the downpour. They had made it halfway through the field without incident, but their luck only had so much allowance.

Rain-outlined warriors only grew bigger as Isála held her breath, kneeling in the cold mud.

Rione pulled her axes from their cradles, the water cascading off the blades. "Be ready," she whispered through the storm.

The moment Rione shifted, a whistle cut through the bass of the downpour.

An arrow crashed into the dirt behind them while several warriors outlined by the rain approached from the south.

If not for the wind and rain changing the arrow's trajectory, the arrow would have found its mark.

Rione grabbed Isála's wrist and pulled her to her feet. Several more arrows wobbled through the storm as they began running, their feet fighting the mud with each step.

For all her talk of peace, Isála could only feel anger. How many needed to die? What amount of blood would quench their thirst? Was her father's blood not enough? Her brother's? Teshun's? If giving up and offering herself would end their need, Isála wouldn't hesitate. But nothing would be enough. They had to be stopped.

She slid to her knees and brushed the long grass with her outstretched hands before turning and exhaling into The Song. Pain emanated from her injury and wrenched her left arm, but anger tempered the worst of it. The River slowed to a ballad, and ice crept over the waterlogged earth between them and their pursuers.

A muffled clatter joined the chaotic noise of the storm as Isála ran to catch up with Rione.

If they meant to kill her, they would have to fight The River too.

Every stride, every hurried breath quaked through her body. Arrows continued to pass erratically through the storm.

The water of the strait joined the chaos of The Song, a deep rhythm too heavy to be moved by the rain.

"We're almost there," Isála screamed.

The pattern of Rione's footfalls shifted, and Isála looked up to find the unassailable warrior tumbling to the ground with an arrow in her back.

"Get up!" Isála yelled.

The warriors were gaining as she tried to pull Rione to her feet.

"Go without me!" Rione pushed Isála's hands away.

"Fuck you. You want to be a martyr? Too fucking bad," Isála said, her nose nearly touching Rione's. "Teshun didn't die to lead the way for you. He died so you could see this through. Get up!"

No matter what Isála had been through in the last span, the expression on Rione's face was the closest she had ever been to death. The older warrior bared her teeth as she pushed herself to her feet.

Isála lent her spirit to the clouds above. Endless potential waited in the collective beads trapped within. She worked through The Song, asking the water to remember the chill of winter.

Small pellets of ice replaced the rain, followed by larger and larger spheres of hail plummeting from the sky. She did her best to direct the heaviest of the assault behind them, but The Song could only twist nature so much.

The chunks of ice thudded into the ground. A sphere caught her in the shoulder, and pain blossomed over her flesh.

As long as she could keep their pursuers from finding their aim, she could endure the pain for the last fifty paces. Hope waited on the shoreline in front of them.

Then, hope broke.

A dozen warriors waited for them, framed by the uneasy waters.

Yesterday, Isála had taken a life. In the throes of defending herself, after losing two fingers, she reached for Mātan's knife and killed her attacker. She hadn't made a decision. Not consciously.

But here and now, she had to decide what mattered. Tension between her ideals and Ennea's well-being stretched, promising to split her in two. Either choice would define her—on this plane or the next—and there would be no going back.

A chill far deeper than what wind and rain could evoke seized her body. She caught sight of the pretty warrior she had seen days before. The warrior she had wondered over like a daydream held a spear in her hands, waiting in line with her compatriots.

So be it, she thought.

The steady rhythm of the Strait of Talmo deepened as she pulled the tide away from the shore. The water fought to return to its resting. It wanted to remain a steady foundation in The Song, but Isāla tore at the undercurrent. The pull of the water receded farther from the rocky bank.

The warriors waiting for them with weapons drawn didn't notice the irregular tide.

"Just keep running," Isāla said.

Her mother probably had plenty of reasons for her decisions. Blood owed blood. Or loyalty to Renēqua. Blessed Mother, it could have been pure ambition.

Maybe it wasn't the actions that made Isāla like or different from her mother. Maybe the reasons behind her actions mattered more.

As waters from the strait receded into the ocean, The River bucked against the unnatural pull.

Everything in nature—everything that dancers could manipulate— sought equilibrium. The waters wanted to return to their rightful place.

The pressure in Isāla's head throbbed, all the while ice pelted her from the sky. She had to wait for the right time, when the waters had enough weight behind them.

"If you have a plan, now would be the time!" Rione yelled.

Twenty paces separated them from the line of warriors when Isāla let go of her hold on the water. It surged forward, claiming the space it once had occupied. The force crashed over the shoreline.

"Blessed fucking Mother!" Rione yelled.

Heavy waters slammed into the waiting warriors, tossing them to the ground. The swell clung to those who had been standing closest and dragged them out into the chaotic waters. The pretty warrior vanished under the white-capped tumult.

As the strait tried to find balance, it spun a handful of warriors about. Desperate faces reached for the surface before the current pulled them back under.

Isála had seen herself in the unnamed Tomakan warrior with the short crown of hair, but they both had chosen their paths. Isála's counterpart and her fellow warriors' fates would be their own now. Spirits would cross. And Isála would have to bear that weight.

The lucky ones clung to the bank, some coughing up water, others searching for lost weapons.

Rione and Isála charged forward and dove into the strait. Arrows pursued them beyond the surface as the angered waters twisted them about, a ferocious cold sinking into their bones.

When they found their way to the surface, Isála's lungs begged for more air, but she didn't have the time. Too many warriors leveled their bows for their blood.

"Hold your breath!" Isála yelled with whatever strength her lungs could muster.

She clung to Rione's arm and dove, dancing with The River's pull. The Song had no end from within the strait, the current thrumming through it.

Motioning The Song to her designs, a rush of force pulled them deeper into the waters and farther from the shore. Pressure tightened and enveloped Isála, but still she continued away from the surface.

They had to put distance between them and the archers.

Shimmers of the moons cut through the darkness. The bubbles of their exhalations trailed in the wake of their movement.

For all the hostility of the waters, The Song had never been so full.

Rione squeezed Isāla's arm with a panic, but Isāla only had to reach into The Song to shift their angle through the water. It pushed them back to the surface.

The hail storm had ceased. Arrows continued to search for them. But from the middle of the strait, they were the safest they had been in days.

They reached their tired arms through the water, drawing themselves closer to the shores of Renēqua.

CHAPTER TWELVE

ISÃLA

Before the nations, small clans gathered to safeguard each other. Those small communities combined or consumed one another. They drew borders around each other and found ways to other the people from different nations. But, in truth, people on opposite sides of these lines are much more similar than they are different. Physical features predominant to one nation or another have more to do with history than they have to do with distinctions between our peoples.

Becoming Tomak, Tomakan Elder Lorni

After days of facing blades and arrows, Isãla sat in a hovel of a room more anxious than ever. The walls were a series of wooden slats. What little sunlight slipped through gave the room a dim glow. Stores of grain and beans had been hastily thrown to the edges of the room to make space for her before the guards closed and latched the door behind them.

Eventually, someone would come. That someone could be her mother, and the thought made her body plead for movement. And still, in defiance of her anxiety, she sat at the edge of the room without Mãtan's knife, the black flag, or the letter.

When the water deposited her and Rione on the rocky shores of Renêqua, she had dragged her injured friend beyond the tideline with the last of her energy. She crumbled to her knees with an emptiness growing inside her. In place of the pain and exhaustion that should have been there, the weight of those who had died for them to reach this moment held her in place.

Rione coughed and spat out water beside her, still face-down prone against the rough beach.

Shouts and clattering noises called from the distance, strangely not mattering.

Isála examined her friend for signs of further injuries. After Rione emptied the water from her lungs, the nearly indestructible warrior lay unmoving save the rise and fall of her chest. Blood softly streamed from around the shaft of the arrow protruding from her back.

Apart from the arrow, Rione had no other visible injuries. Still, her eyes stared off into the distance, glassy and dull, lacking the intensity that defined her.

Beneath the descending light of The Daughters, a group of warriors still too far away to count rushed towards them. This was why they had come. The weight that pulled at her spirit would be for nothing if she failed now.

Abject terror jolted Isála upright. The missive—her reason for this journey. The leather binding had been designed to safeguard the paper, but she had just crossed the Strait of Talmo after running through a torrential downpour.

She yanked the missive from inside her robes and ripped the thread sealing the leather pouch. As she unfolded the layers of hide, her breathing grew shallow. She should have read its contents before crossing that damn field.

Her hands shook, holding the final layer of tanned hide protecting the missive. If she had come all this way only to deliver a water-damaged piece of parchment, she wouldn't be able to live with herself.

As soon as she revealed the letter within, she collapsed to her knees. She drew her finger across the dry piece of folded-up parchment.

After everything, the letter seemed so insignificant.

Before she could peel it open, she stopped herself. It would be better if she didn't know where the conclave would be held. The answer could only seem too lowly for all that it needed to be.

The Clan had asked her to deliver this missive and nothing more.

A dozen green-robed warriors approached with their weapons drawn. At least, they seemed to be slower to draw back their bows than the Tomakans. But no one with any understanding of the war would doubt their ability or willingness to kill.

Isāla re-wrapped the missive and untied the black flag still cinched at her waist with a calmness that the moment hadn't earned. The waterlogged cloth fought her, but eventually, it hung in her hand.

A simple black flag like this had started this march towards peace. Nearly three turns ago, a nomad had waved a black flag to parlay with the Astileans, and an archer struck him down. The forgiveness of the nomad's loved ones humbled Astile and brought them into talks with the Clan.

The morbid history of the symbol aside, the Clan had done much under the banner of a black flag. Isāla lifted it in her hands, doing the best to catch the wind with the water-saturated cloth.

A breathy whistle crept into the heavy silence.

Rione had shifted to bring the whistle to her lips. The hollow length of ashburn emitted an unsteady rhythm of tones, which didn't carry far.

Certain moments had the ability to strip the veneer from the world and bare its truth. Since the moment Isāla had laid eyes on her, Rione had been immoveable—confident in every step taken and word uttered. Now, as she lingered on the edge of The Mist, fumbling with a whistle, she seemed undeniably fragile.

Part of Isāla had understood how fragile people were. No amount of bravado or chest-thumping could hide that. But a piece of her had seen warriors as removed from everyone else.

Bending down, she took the whistle from Rione and imitated the pattern while waving the flag the best she could with an injured hand. It all probably looked laughable—waving a water-logged flag and hooting away on a whistle at the edge of the strait.

Better laughable than threatening, she thought.

A single Renêquan warrior approached them as the others brandished their bows. He was nearing his middle turns, and carried himself with a baring that assumed respect rather than demanded it. Dark stubble lined his passive expression. This was one of Isâla's people.

"Who are cha? Wha tis it cha want?" he asked, with a thicker accent than Isâla had heard in years.

"The Clan sends us in the name of peace," Isâla said, not daring to try her unpracticed mother tongue. "We seek an audience with General Jerîka. I am her daughter, Isâla."

The warrior's shoulders fell as he looked incredulously at her. "Cha lies need work, youngin."

"Bring her my uncle's knife," Isâla said, gesturing to the blade on her hip. "But please do it quickly. My friend needs a healer."

The warrior removed the knife from Isâla's sheath, looking from it to Rione's prone body before gesturing to his compatriots.

As the group of warriors swept in around Isâla and Rione, stripping them of their remaining weapons, her numbness dissipated. She would have to confront the woman who gave her away twenty-three turns past.

The hours moved slowly in the storeroom as Isâla waited for the door to open. If The Blessed Mother were kind, Rione was still on this side of The Mist, fighting to stay alive.

The River mimicked Isâla's trepidation with layers of timid tones weaving one over another.

Regardless of whether her mother and the Renêquan elders attended the conclave, Isâla's world had forever changed because of the past several days. She had too many questions. Life and the Clan teachings had fallen out of harmony. No matter how pretty their ideas were, Rione had been right. If not for violence, they would never have had this chance for peace.

The door creaked open, filling the floor with sunlight. Dust particles danced in Sokan's beams.

Her mother looked nothing like the woman in Isála's dreams.

General Jeríka's heavy boots dimpled the wood planks as she entered the room. Plumes of gray hair bloomed about her temples before fading to the rich black curls covering her head in a short, neat cut. The turns had stolen the joy from her. In Isála's dreams, her cheekbones pulled her face into an unending smile.

That smile was nowhere to be seen.

This stranger stood at the doorway with sunlight pooling around her, staring at Isála. Her green robes wrapped over her shoulders in a way that highlighted the bulk of her chest. Looking upon her, no one could question her warrior's prowess.

"Cha shouldna come here," Jeríka said as she closed the door behind her. Something about how her accent curled around her words—the way Isála should have sounded—made Isála feel even more disconnected from this woman.

"Where is my friend?"

"Ta Tomakan woman? She'll live." The General's lips curled in a scowl. "Cha shouldna be here."

Twenty-three turns of resentment grew sour in Isála's gut. "Where should I be, mother? I was born here. This is my home too, right? Or did that change when you abandoned me?"

"Don take tat tone wit me. No one abandoned cha."

"You don't get to order me around." Isála pushed herself to her feet and found it odd to stand at an even height with her mother. "I'm not one of your warriors. You saw to that."

"Tat what cha wanted? Cha wanted ta be a warrior?" Jérika sucked her teeth at the notion. "Is tat what cha came here ta say? I saved cha from ta war."

The River chanted a chorus of threats in crescendo—a series of waves growing harsher with each crash against the shoreline.

"And you ran back to it. You don't think I have lost people to the bloodshed? I have, but when I did, I didn't have my mother to help me through it. Tell yourself what you have to, but don't lie to me. You stayed for yourself!"

Jĕrika took a deep breath and stared death at Isála. The woman who had spent her life giving orders and putting people in their place remained where she stood, her fist shaking at her side. The silence stretched like too little leather drawn over a drumhead, ready to tear in twine.

"Cha had Mătan." Her voice shivered.

"When my father and brother died, my mother left too," Isála said, her words slow but steady. "Mătan couldn't save me from that. I needed you."

"Someone had ta claim ta blood tey took from us! Someone had ta fight for our people!"

Every warrior, no matter the nation they fought, had said the same thing. Whenever Isála'd had the opportunity to speak with one, they all created a righteous story for themselves. It had become the reason her mother had given her in her dreams. But hearing it from Jĕrika felt odd. A part of her hoped her mother would differ from the others.

"Has any of the blood over the last twenty-three turns brought them back—made things better?"

"Cha ave too much of cha father in ya. Cha would've never lasted this long as a warrior."

"You don't know anything about the person I am or what I am capable of." Isála saw Mătan's knife dangling from her mother's belt, and the shadow dancer's face flashed in front of her. She had already proven the lengths she would go for what she believed.

Jĕrika followed Isála's gaze to the knife and pulled it from its sheath. "Do cha know where tis knife came from? It was cha father's, and I asked Matan ta give it ta cha when cha were old enough."

The knife turned back and forth in Jĕrika's hands, and the woman became something closer to familiar as the harshness slipped from her expression.

"Cha father, Blessed Mother hold him, gave me tis knife when I first joined ta army. Tis was long before cha were born. He didn believe in ta wars. Said tings like blood owed forgiveness and all tat.

"Still, he gave me tis knife. Cha father's father tempered ta blade, and cha father carved ta hilt." Her fingers ran over the wood as she spoke. "Do cha rememba him?"

"Barely remember you, to be honest."

Jerīka's lips rose into a tight, pained grin. "Don even speak propa, do cha?"

"I'm not here to reminisce," Isāla said, not intending the hurt from her mother's comment to color her voice. "Did you read the Clan's message?"

"Ta Clan been sending envoys for near two turns. I heard tem out, but I neva agreed ta no peace talks. Some tings can't be forgiven, and some people can't be trusted—no matta what cha father used ta say."

"Maybe this isn't about forgiveness. Maybe this is about deciding to take care of the people still in The Waking. How many more broken families does Renēqua need? Or do orphans make better warriors?"

"Tat's enough!" The fierce warrior broke past the pained mother, and Jērika's presence loomed all the larger. "Cha can be angry as cha want at me, but no one says noting bout my warriors."

"How many of them have families they may never see again? How many of them will get the chance to be there for their children? If you care so much about your warriors or your people, give them a chance to live for something other than blood."

The woman in front of Isāla was several women fighting to become one—the grieving wife and mother, the guilty parent, the wrathful warrior, the exhausted general, and the lost Renēquan. As fragile as Rione had been on the shore, in this moment, Isāla's mother was infinitely more so.

"Is this the life you want to live, Mother? Is that what you want for your people? For me? I had to kill people to make it here. Something I promised myself I would never do. I hate myself for it—no matter how necessary it might have been. My friend, Teshun, Rione's brother, died to get us here. This has to end. Blessed Mother, we can be better than this."

"Tey killed cha father! Tey killed cha brother!"

"Blood won't bring them back. But you could be my mother again." As Isála said the words, she was surprised by how much she meant them. After spending her life trying to be anything but her mother's daughter, that was ultimately all she wanted to be.

Jērika took a step closer, her gaze finding Isála's injured hand, the waterlogged fabric doing nothing more than hiding the grotesqueness of the wound.

Finally close enough to touch, Jērika held her open palm out as a request. Isála hesitated, then placed her hand in her mother's. A wave of sorrow swept across Jērika's face as she gently unwrapped the fabric.

The General must have seen hundreds if not thousands of injuries before, but she held her breath as if this were the first. Sand and dried blood mingled with the remnants of the poultice, obscuring the gore of the injury.

"We will get tis seen ta," Jērika said, emotion fighting with her stoic words.

"We could build this country up instead of tearing others down." Isála pulled her hand back, cradling it with her other. "You could teach me what this land means to you. Maybe it could mean something to me, too. But the fighting has to stop first."

"Wha do cha want from me?"

"I want you to choose me over your anger. I want you to fight for something other than vengeance," Isála said. "Take away the borders and these wars are just a lot of people trying to balance grief with blood."

"Cha don know noting about it!" Jerīka yelled, clutching the knife until her knuckles turned pale.

"I know what these wars have cost me. I should have grown up here with my family. We shouldn't be strangers. You have no idea how many times I have mourned the life that was stolen from me," Isála said, the pitch of her voice sharpening.

The door burst open behind Jerīka, and a young warrior stood in the gap. "General, Elder Utăn's here. He's requessin cha presence."

"Tell ta elder I'll be tere in a moment."

The warrior nodded and closed the door as he left.

"What are you going to tell the elder?" Isála asked, hope threading through her voice.

Jérika studied Isála, pausing at her cradled injury. "I've neva backed down from a fight, not even words aroun a table," she said. "I can't promise anyting, but ta elders listen ta me."

Tears crested over Isála's eyelids. "Thank you."

"Cha may ave cha father's ideas, but cha got cha mother's fight." Jérika reached out to touch Isála's cheek and a pained smile curled her lips. "I'll ave someone come by ta check on tat hand."

The door closed, and once again, Isála found herself alone.

Her mother had been everything she feared she would be: a stubborn warrior, a grieving mother and wife, an imperfect reflection of herself. And after meeting her, Isála was too tired for all the thoughts and emotions fighting for her attention.

She had experienced the bloodiest days of her life in exchange for a few minutes of conversation. And now it was over.

Nothing had been promised. So much work remained. But hope no longer felt like a fool's quest.

EPILOGUE

ISÁLA

Isála massaged her left hand to calm the insistent itch from her wound. The pain reminded her of Teshun in a bittersweet way. Even if she were tempted to forget their journey north, all she had to do was look down at her hand. Hopefully, time would sooth the bitterness of her permanent reminder.

Her supplies lay strewn across the swept dirt floor of her tent. None of it seemed necessary. No one had a missive or a mission for her. No enemies lurked in the forest with brandished blades. She simply had to travel with the land as she had for over two decades.

Only now, there would be no war to contend with.

The canopy shook as Mátan drew back the hides covering the entrance to her tent, much like he had nearly a season past.

"You don't have to go. We could use your help. If the Jani—I'm
still not used to that. If the Clan is going to become the nation it was
proclaimed to be, we will need people like you."

"I'll be back, Uncle. You know I will be, but I have to do this. Part of
me is lost until I get to know my mother," she said. "Plus, I need ta work
on my proper tongue."

"Blessed Mother, you sure do. What was that?" His smile spread,
making him the young man who had taken her in all those turns ago.

"Do you think we'll get along?"

"You and Jeríka are two of the most wonderfully stubborn people I
know. I pray The Mother watches over Renêqua," he said before his smile
settled into a serious expression. "You and her are the most important
people in my life. Both of you are lucky to have the chance to know each
other. Just remember that."

She shot up from the middle of her scattered possessions and crashed
into Mãtan's arms. "Thank you for being who I needed you to be."

"You made me proud, little one." He kissed her brow. "Wherever I am,
you have a home."

He helped her finish packing, insisting she take more than necessary.
Though she stopped him before it became obscene—nomads traveled
light after all, and she would always be clan, no matter where she laid her
bedroll.

As she hefted her pack and her new staff, Mãtan remained on the dirt
floor. "Give her time, Isãla. Give yourself time, too."

She nodded and left him to his thoughts. The lighter weight of her
ironoak staff threw her off balance still, but she would get used to it.
With time, anything can become known, or so she hoped.

The whole of the Clan had been busy ever since the Conclave of
Spirits, as it had come to be known, had ended. Some had decided to
return to their homelands and make lives for themselves, rebuilding what
they had left behind. Others, like Mãtan, had decided to stay amongst
the Clan, now formally the borderless nation of the Jani.

Some changes had come quickly. Standing armies were dissolved. Borders were opened, at least in theory. And trade had begun to connect the nations once again.

However, blood was a hard thing to forget. It would take time to heal the wounds the nations had inflicted upon each other. So, whilst the nations rebuilt themselves, the Jani had committed to rebuilding Ennea and the relationships between her people.

Isála approached the small tent at the edge of the Clan's encampment. "Coming in," she said, pushing the furs away from the opening.

"Water dancer, one day you are going to learn a hard lesson about bursting in on a warrior," Rione said from her bedroll with one hand on an onyx axe.

"I'm leaving."

Rione released the axe and stood up, wincing as she moved. The arrow hadn't struck any major organs, but it had scraped along her backbone, making most movements painful.

"I know better than to try to convince you otherwise," Rione said, bending over a sack resting against the tent. "Hold on a moment. There's something I need to give you."

"I have everything I need, Rione. My pack is full."

As Rione turned around, a thin shiny black blade rested in her hands—one of Teshun's throwing daggers. "Whether you intend to use it or not, you should have this. Carry Tesh's spirit with you a bit longer."

"I don't need this to remember Teshun."

"No, I know, but I want you to have it. So stop giving me grief and take the damn thing."

The thin blade sent a chill through Isála's arms as Rione placed it in her hand. "Do you think it will last?" Isála asked.

"My brother's blades don't fade that easily."

"That's not what I meant. This peace—do you think it will last?"

"Blessed fucking Mother, I don't know. I don't make the decisions around here," Rione said, then her tone dropped. "I hope so. Might be nice to go without bloodshed for a bit."

"The mighty Rione hanging up her axes?"

"I never said anything like that. But maybe we were both right in a way. Hopefully, I won't need them anymore."

Isála reached out with both hands and Rione returned the gesture. As Isála clutched Rione's right hand between both of hers, she felt phantoms of her missing fingers join the embrace. They tingled like memory taking form, burning in a way that was becoming familiar.

"Look out for yourself, water dancer."

"You too, Rione."

With her goodbyes said, Isála packed away Teshun's knife. Nomadic life had suited her for a time, but change was on the wind. The River sang a melody of sweeping waters curving through the bend.

Peace would mean far more work than war ever had been.

The Great Spirits

The Shadow: The first of the Great Spirits, known for her wisdom. She blesses her descendants with the ability to manipulate shadows.

The River: The second of the Great Spirits, known for their patience, and twin to The Flame. They bless their descendants with the ability to manipulate water.

The Flame: The third of the Great Spirits, known for their strength, and twin to The River. They bless their descendants with the ability to manipulate fire.

The Mountain: The fourth of the Great Spirits, known for her constant support. She blesses her descendants with the ability to manipulate the earth.

 **THE WIND:** The fifth of the Great Spirits, known for his foresight. He blesses his descendants with the ability to manipulate the air.

 **THE SEED:** The sixth of the Great Spirits, known for his forgiveness. He blesses his descendants with the ability to manipulate plant life.

 **THE THIEF/THE BALANCE:** The seventh of the Great Spirits, known for her pursuit of power or equity depending on whose story you read. She blesses her descendants with the ability to borrow other dancers' abilities.

Glossary

Chani cloth: A light cloth of woven silk. Before the invasion, good chani cloth was worth a goat in trade.

Common tongue: As the nations developed from tribes and villages, disparate languages and dialects began to merge, resulting in a shared language referred to as common tongue.

Conclave of Spirits: Throughout the Hundred-Turn War, citizens of each nation sought peace from the fighting, taking on a nomadic lifestyle. Eventually, a large group of the nomads representing each nation brought together a meeting of the four nations, where they negotiated an end to the fighting. This was also the origin of the fifth nation, the Jani.

Dancer: An Ennean who was gifted with the ability to hear The Song and wield one, or in rare cases two, of the Great Spirits' powers. Also known as children of Ennea or spirit-marked.

Daemontale: A make-believe story told to pass down lessons to children.

ENNEA/THE MOTHER: Ennea is the genesis of life. She is the land and mother to the moons and the sun, the spirits, and the people.

GREAT SPIRITS: Ennea created seven spirits which gave form to The Waking and later gave pieces of their gifts to people in the form of The Song.

HALLOW: A shelter built using The Song and the Great Spirits.

KANA: Ennea's second daughter, the first moon. This also became a term of respect for a mentor and teacher.

LODESTONE: The Jani raised these naturally magnetic stones across Ennea as peaceful meeting places during the Hundred Turns War. Traditionally, Enneas relinquish their weapons to the magnetic pull of the stone while they meet.

MOON: A measurement of time based on the cycles of the moons, approximately thirty days long. When Toka disappears from the sky every third span, it marks a new moon.

SPAN: A measurement of time equivalent to ten days.

SPIRIT-BOUND: An Ennean who is unable to hear The Song. Their spirit is bound to their body and to The Waking.

SOKAN: Ennea's first daughter, the giver, and the sun.

THE MIST: The spiritual plane.

THE SONG: Energy in The Mist seeps through the barrier between planes into The Waking. Dancers have the ability to hear a portion of this energy representing their great spirit ancestor(s). This allows dancers to access the power of their spirit ancestors.

THE WAKING: The physical plane.

TOKA: Ennea's third daughter, the second moon. This also became a term of respect for a mentee and student.

TURN: A unit of time measurement equivalent to four seasons, twelve moons, or approximately three hundred sixty days.

TWICE-MARKED: A dancer who is gifted with the ability to wield two of the Great Spirits' power.

NOTE FROM THE AUTHOR

––––––––––

Don't Bloody the Black Flag is a prequel novella set two hundred years or turns before the events of the Malitu series. Ennea is a place that is dear to me, and I wanted to explore one of the most defining time periods of its history. The Hundred Turn War created a nation, led to the isolation of another nation, and taught Enneans a lesson about the damage that violence can do to a people and their cultures.

This novella was an opportunity for me to explore the philosophical contradictions within the Jani, or as they are referred to at the beginning of this book, the Clan. They are a people made up of refugees and war-deserters who value non-violence and a commitment to The Mother—the land—as their primary tenets. Questions arise: what happens when non-violence becomes inaction and what happens when violence creates a path towards peace?

Within any social movement there are questions about the use of violence in dismantling oppression. I have wrestled with these questions myself and continue to wrestle with them. In fantasy or when watching situations from afar, the answers may seem easy. However, as a white man with many privileges in his life, I have never been forced to find out these answers for myself.

My voice can and should only be a small part of this conversation that should center BIPOC voices first and foremost. If you have not read authors of color who are creating amazing works in speculative fiction that engage with violence and resistance, I encourage you to start. There are countless important voices to add to your to-be-read (TBR) list. Below, I have listed some authors I have read and enjoyed.

Tomi Adeyemi, Octavia Butler, C.L. Clark, Tracy Deonn, Justina Ireland, N.K. Jemisin, R.F. Kuang, Fonda Lee, L. Penelope, Tatiana Obey, Nnedi Okorafor, PhD, Kritika H. Rao, Rebecca Roanhorse, Andrea Stewart, Moses Ose Utomi, ML Wang, Evan Winters

When creating the world of Ennea, I was not looking to tell anyone else's story for them. While aspects of Ennean history, culture, and philosophy contain similarities to real world cultures and people, Ennea is not based on any specific group of people. The questions around violence in Don't Bloody the Black Flag are sadly applicable to the state-led violence within and between countries throughout the world.

Artists who are privileged within systems of oppression, like myself, must educate ourselves and take care when addressing these subject matters. Even with that said, I have and will make mistakes along the way. I will continue to do my best to remedy my mistakes to the best of my ability. I am dedicated to listening, learning, and continuing to improve.

I have openly dedicated myself to take accountability for any harm my books cause marginalized communities, and will continue to do my best be a part of this important conversation.

I believe in and love this story, and I am responsible for its content and impact.

Thank you for the opportunity to tell this story.

James Lloyd Dulin

MORE BOOKS BY JAMES LLOYD DULIN

No Heart For A Thief
Malitu Book One

No Safe Haven
Malitu Book Two

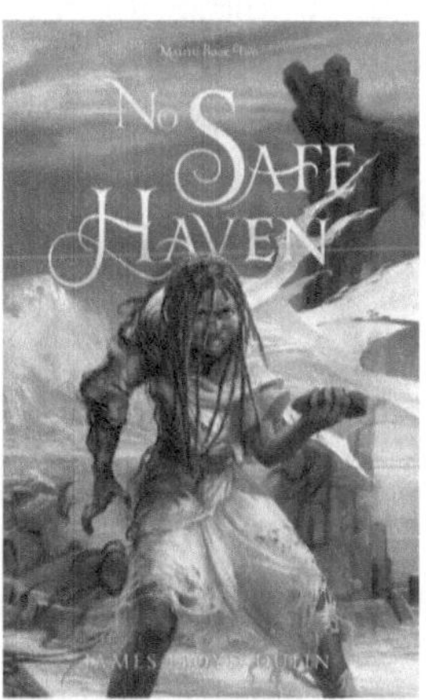

ACKNOWLEDGEMENTS

The indie publishing world has become such an important community in my life. People within this community have affirmed me, held me accountable, supported me, challenged me, and made me a better writer.

Though I cannot thank everyone, I want to take the time to recognize some people who helped me with this story.

The first and the last people to thank will always be my family. Aneicka, Sonny, and Dominic make this world worth it. Without them, I wouldn't be able to put these stories on the page. It may be fantasy, but it requires humanity, and they are vital to mine.

Don't Bloody the Black Flag was the first time I ever attempted a novella. It would be completely unreadable without the help of my beta readers and editor. Thank you to João Silva, Joseph John Lee, Angelicka Morgan, Katherine D. Graham, and Sarah Chorn.

Books are more than the words better the cover. A cover can draw readers and tell a story on its own. Martin Mottet did an incredible job with the cover art for Don't Bloody the Black Flag, and my brother, Michael Dulin, made the art into a beautifully designed cover.

ACKNOWLEDGEMENTS

To my readers, I never thought that I would have this many people pick up my stories. I am not a best-selling author, but that doesn't matter. You have given me the chance to tell these stories because these words are nothing if I am screaming them into the void. You give these characters life. Thank you.

If I can ask you to help me take this one step further, please review this book on Amazon, Goodreads, and any other platform you might use. Reviews are the lifeblood for self-published authors. Reviews encourage others to give a book a try, and I want to share this book with as many people as I can.